PUFFIN PLUS

JANEY

One good look's worth half a street's start, Lou always told her. *Take your time outside, girl, 'cos there's tons of it in Borstal.*

Janey knew it didn't pay to make mistakes when her bullying stepfather Lou was sitting in a car just round the corner. She'd been sure the house was empty before breaking in – but there, on the floor, was what looked like a dead body. It was only the thought of what Lou would do that kept her from screaming. But then she heard cries for help and realized it wasn't a dead body: it was an old woman who had fallen over and was lying helpless on the floor. Janey knew what she should do – run: Lou's training told her that. But there was something about the old woman that made her stay. And that something was just the beginning of Janey's desperate struggle to break away from Lou's violent domination, and the life of crime that lay ahead of her.

A compelling, up-to-the minute story set in the streets of south-east London.

Bernard Ashley was born in Woolwich, South London, in 1935. He grew up in London and in the Medway towns and began his teaching career in Gravesend, Kent. He is now a head teacher with the Inner London Education Authority, living in Charlton. His wife is also a teacher and they have three sons. He enjoys the theatre and watching football and also travelling abroad.

Some other books by Bernard Ashley

ALL MY MEN
BREAK IN THE SUN
DINNER LADIES DON'T COUNT
DODGEM
HIGH PAVEMENT BLUES
I'M TRYING TO TELL YOU
A KIND OF WILD JUSTICE
RUNNING SCARED
TERRY ON THE FENCE
THE TROUBLE WITH DONOVAN CROFT

BERNARD ASHLEY

JANEY

PUFFIN BOOKS

Puffin Books, Penguin Books Ltd, Harmondsworth, Middlesex, England
Viking Penguin Inc., 40 West 23rd Street, New York, New York 10010, U.S.A.
Penguin Books Australia Ltd, Ringwood, Victoria, Australia
Penguin Books Canada Limited, 2801 John Street, Markham, Ontario, Canada L3R 1B4
Penguin Books (N.Z.) Ltd, 182–190 Wairau Road, Auckland 10, New Zealand

First published by Julia MacRae Books 1985
Published in Puffin Books 1986
Reprinted 1987

Printed and bound in Great Britain by
Cox & Wyman Ltd, Reading

*I should like to acknowledge
the generous help given by
Julia Dalton, Brian Hall and Marion Orton*

CONTENTS

PART ONE: AUTUMN INTO WINTER

Chapter One, page 9
Chapter Two, page 19
Chapter Three, page 41
Chapter Four, page 53
Chapter Five, page 65
Chapter Six, page 85
Chapter Seven, page 105

PART TWO: SPRING INTO SUMMER

Chapter Eight, page 119
Chapter Nine, page 136
Chapter Ten, page 155

PART ONE

AUTUMN INTO WINTER

"Janey? What you doin' after school?"

Janey gripped hard with her feet and her free hand. "Eh?" The top of the ropes was a funny old place for a chat. But then Mary Richards was a funny old friend. Always making some plans. She'd stop at her own wedding, halfway down the church, and fix up where she was going to meet you after the honeymoon. She always had to know the arrangements, did Mary.

"Robbing a bank. Can't come out."

Janey made the finishing shape they'd been told to: Mary did the same: white and black, reaching for the gym ceiling.

"That's good, girls. Janey, a bit more pride."

Janey stuck her nose in the air.

"Only I forgot to tell you. My mum's out. We can go in the front room."

Janey shifted her hold. So what? Her mum had been out two years: she could go to the moon for all anyone cared.

"What about tomorrow, then?"

"Yeah, if you like." Janey went down; left Mary up there. It was rotten, she liked going home with Mary; but after school she'd got to go out with Lou. It was one of those things you couldn't get out of. No way. She stood to attention. When he'd made his mind up to something there wasn't any saying no to Lou. Shame! You had a good meal at Mary's. And a good laugh. It was what helped keep her going sometimes.

But she definitely had to go with Lou and that was all there was to it. No good moaning. That never did the least bit of good.

ONE

The car drove slowly past the house they were going to rob and pulled into the kerb twenty metres or so further on. Janey twisted in her seat.

"D'you see that big window it's got? Like a church, pictures in the glass?" She had to take an interest, be the partner, or he went all moody.

Lou Tanner looked at the house behind its wild privet hedge. "Eh? Don't start goin' holy on me, girl! All I wanna know about windows is, do they open when you push 'em?"

Janey rocked the car, still looking. "Not the pictures, stupid; don't know about the pictures – but that lead holdin' them together. That fetches a bit, don't it?"

The man gave her one of his looks, the 'you little madam' stare he'd passed on to her after her mother had gone. "You're no more'n a totter at heart," he told her. "Bit o' lead like that wouldn't keep me in matches." He looked around, at the house, up and down the empty road. "Go on, give 'em a knock. We've been past three times and there's not a sign o' life. Hundred to one they're out." He looked hard into what there was of a wing mirror. "But if you do get an answer, don' get involved, you hear me? None of your little-orphan-Annie 'ard luck stories. Just ask for your school jumble an' get off out of it." Janey shoved the near-side back door. "An' if you cock it up this time I swear I'll 'ave this belt off to you!"

The girl snorted. "What, an' let that belly out? You wouldn't have an 'and to spare!"

He threw a clout at her, but she'd gone, shot over the road and started to run along by the dusty hedge. She knew the game, he didn't have to tell her. She'd done it often enough, hadn't she? He wouldn't know, but you *had* to spin your story

9

out, tell them what it was all supposed to be in aid of or they'd soon start getting suspicious. The lazy fat slob, he only made a move when the tricky stuff was done, when he knew the house was empty: he never took the chance of being asked a load of questions.

The gate was stuck part-way open, with a rusty curve on the black and white tiles where it rubbed the front path. The over-grown hedge cut the opening to half, and Janey gave it a quick eye for spiders before she slid through the gap. Inside, where she couldn't be seen from the road, she stopped and looked around her. *One good look's worth half a street's start*, Lou always told her. *Take your time outside, girl, 'cos there's tons of it in Borstal.* He should know! She was standing in grass like their own, up to her knees and smelling of cat muck. A fruit tree gone wild swayed against the wall of the house, its rub showing how bright the bricks had been when the place was built. A wall-flower grew out from a drain pipe. Path tiles were missing and the pattern was broken up. It was all let go, Janey thought, you wouldn't think anyone lived here, if you didn't know what to look for. But the porch was clean with no cobwebs, and a sparkling milk bottle stood neat at the side of the door. No, this wasn't any old dosser's kip, she could tell that. Someone did live here all right, which meant there was definitely stuff inside. That should please him, then. He'd been right for once.

She looked up at the stained-glass window. It was even bigger up close. From where she was just underneath she could see that it reached from the landing to the ceiling. And it was all one picture, like a land in the Bible, all mountains and twisty trees and people bending over in the fields. Quite nice when you saw it up close – but, well, out of place round here: a bit like seeing a flash car outside the fish and chip. And he was wrong, the fat slob: there was tons of lead in it, if the window got smashed.

She stopped looking round and walked up towards the house. Her scruffy reflection in a downstairs window checked her for just a moment: she was supposed to have been sent from the school, so she did up another button on her frock and ruffled

10

the curls of her hair before she put her best do-gooding look on her face and marched innocently up to the front door.

The bell had a small light in it behind a card, but the printed name was hard to make out with the fading of the ink. All the same, Janey could read what she needed to know: the electricity was still on: which meant she'd been right; the place definitely hadn't been left to the mice and the spiders, and she'd better keep well on her toes.

She put her thumb to the button and leaned on it; heard a straight ring coming from somewhere a long way back in the house, while she squinted through the frosted glass of the door for some slight crinkle in the hall.

Nothing. Hard as she tried she couldn't hear any other noises; and the pattern in the glass stayed just the same, the only moving shape her own white reflection going all ways at once. She knocked, and heard it echo. Still nothing. So she did what she always saved till last and looked through the letter box.

No string, no key dangling.

The hallway she saw was long, wide and bare, with plain wooden squares instead of lino. The wallpaper was raised up in a pattern and painted over white, there was a barometer and some big brown pictures hanging on the wall, and by the stairs a mac and a hat made a hallstand look like someone was standing there watching. It gave her a bit of a jump. A clothes brush lay like a dead hedgehog on the floor and a door down the hall was half open.

It all told a story, easy to read when you'd done as much of this as Janey had. Going by the coat, there was one old girl who'd probably popped out to the shops or round to some club – while the cat had had a game with the brush up and down the hall. It looked a likely place for Lou all right; experience told her that old girls like this often had all sorts of treasures tucked away – stuff they didn't even know they'd got. Valuable stuff. But before Janey went running back for him there was a bit more checking she had to do.

11

She left the porch and sidled along the front of the house, trying to squint through a heavy net which hung at one of the big bay windows. Because you had to be careful. One time they'd gone into a house which looked empty and found an old man in the front room ill in bed. She could still remember Lou apologising, offering to pour him a drink – and the scared, weak croaks from the poor old bloke. But this net was too thick and the room was too dark for her to see anything inside. She went on to the side gate: as there was one, she'd be stupid not to check round the back. Better safe than sorry, she thought, before she let Lou loose on the place.

She tried the latch, thumbed it loudly just like someone with nothing to hide; she pushed, and the thing gave, opened with a squeak and swung her in with its weight. Janey let herself be taken. Why not? She was only after jumble, doing a good turn for the school: no need to look like a crook, was there? But there was still no seeing in through any windows. There were heavy nets at all of them, and the back door, peeling its paint like sunburn, had frosted glass in all its small frames.

Janey knocked at it and hurt her knuckles. "'Ey! Anyone in?" she tried. She put her head to the door and listened hard for any hint of a sound; she tried to feel with the side of her face for any give which could mean another door had opened somewhere inside – one of the signs, like the smells of coffee or burning toast, which told her whether people were in or out. But there was nothing here. All the same, she waited; she still wasn't going to jump too quickly; she'd been tripped up before by the length of time it took old people to get to the door.

While she stood and counted up to a hundred, she ran a professional eye over the back of the house. There was a drainpipe going up, but it was nowhere near to a handy bedroom, and the kitchen window was shut tight. But what was that, up above the french doors going into the back living room? A small window was open a crack for air, propped out on a metal stay. Well, that was a bit of luck. Definitely a way in, but it was much too small for Lou's fat gut to manage. He'd probably send her, then get her to walk through and open the back door, save himself the sweat of five minutes with a steel bar.

Janey looked up at it. Well, why not do it now, save all the to-ing and fro-ing? It'd be one less thing for people to see, just waving at Lou from a window upstairs. And no sense hanging about out here for ever: she'd given the oldest old girl time to show herself. So, just one last check on the back door. Janey pulled down the handle, ready to let it go again and double back to the french doors. But the thing gave! The door moved, hadn't been locked at all, and it swung open as if someone was at it from the other side. *What the* . . . ! Janey swallowed, cocked her head, overcame the sudden dipping in her belly and put on her politest face. " 'Ello?"

But the kitchen was empty, there was no-one there to see her big brown eyes and her tilted chin. Just a drop-leaf table, a couple of metal chairs, a cup and saucer draining, and a steady tapping in the sink. Plus potted plants on the window sill and a line of school photographs leaning along the dresser, all of the same girl, getting older. A gran's house, Janey thought, definitely – like her own gran's had been, till she'd died.

She edged round the door and shut it, quietly, giving it time to settle against the jamb before she left it.

The old girl had probably done what a lot of them do. Got forgetful, gone out the back way and forgot to lock the door. Or else she'd left it open on purpose, only nipped out for five minutes – because the side gate hadn't been locked, had it? Well, there was still time to do what they'd come for if they were quick. There'd better be! she thought. An evening with Lou if they went home empty-handed again didn't bear thinking about.

Janey crossed the kitchen on her toes and flattened herself against the inside door: she listened once more: and with the caution of a safe-breaker she turned the knob and opened the door wide, set it back gently against the passage wall.

It was dim out there. Not that Janey minded that very much,

13

she'd got used to moving about without daring to show a light. All she had to do now was get up the stairs and wave out of a front window. Half a minute, that'd take. Less.

She took two more tiptoes – and suddenly she froze rigid. Sticking out from the room on her right was a pair of feet in shiny slippers, all twisted and still. Someone dead, it had to be! God, she'd always dreaded this happening. It made her want to scream the house down. But in the last instant Lou's training got hold of her. Little fool! That'd bring next door running for sure! She shoved her fist in her mouth to choke on the sound instead. Just slide past the feet – and don't look at them! Get out, quick and quiet, and don't even think about what horrible thing could be lying behind that door.

She closed her eyes and flattened herself as thin as she could along the wall. All she could hear was the sound of her heart as its thumping threatened to throw her closer to the feet. Until she came level with the door . . .

"Help me! Help me, please!"

Janey stumbled. Her eyes opened but she still couldn't see beyond the edge of the door. The voice was very faint but it was clear, not frightening at all really, once it had spoken.

"There is someone there, isn't there? Is it from the church?"

Janey wanted to run, back the way she'd come, out through the kitchen and round to Lou.

"Be my angel! I'm stuck down here otherwise!"

But there was something about the voice – a ring she knew – and suddenly there was no way Janey could run. How long had her nan been down on the floor before the neighbour saw the milk and knocked a window in?

Carefully, she edged her eyes around the door and saw an old woman lying there; stuck on her side, with both her arms reaching out for an empty armchair. Her chin was down in her chest as she twisted herself awkwardly to look up at the doorway.

"You're a little angel from heaven and you've saved my life."

"Yeah?"

14

"I've been down here since I don't know when. Luvaduck, I hope I'm not showing you my drawers."

Janey had to smile. She looked down. She was, as it happened, long, shiny things that came right down to her knees. "Yeah, pink," she told her.

"Then it's Friday. Pink to make the boys wink, Tuesdays and Fridays, and I know it's not Tuesday. Come on, love, give us a hand up."

Janey took it all in, an old woman, well dressed, with a round face, grey hair, and one of those walking gadgets fallen over out of her reach.

"Just look at me. Dropped the clothes brush and tipped over. Helpless! Hours, I've been down here. I shall wet myself in a minute, then I'll feel a fool. Come on, lovie, give us a hand up." She was struggling again, getting a bit impatient now that help was at hand.

And it was too late for Janey to go. There was no turning her back now: no pretending she hadn't seen the fix the old girl was in. Besides, doing what she had to do with Lou didn't mean she couldn't help someone who was in a state, did it?

"Hold tight, then." Janey went into the room, stepped over the old woman, took hold of her hands and started trying to drag her over towards the armchair. Strewth! She was bigger than she'd thought.

"I know I'm a weight; two ton Tessie! But I've got no push in my legs. Ouch! Oh, you're a ... good ... girl ..."

Janey had no breath for talk. Moving the old woman was as much as she could cope with. She strained and she pulled, nearly burst a blood vessel as she dragged her arms out of their sockets to get the dead weight across the carpet.

"That's it, love, ouch, ooh, that's it ... once more ... heave away ..." And with an enormous effort Janey did it. Somehow she got the old woman close enough to the chair to grab it for herself; when, with a surprising strength in the old arms, the woman turned herself over and pulled herself up to lie sprawling sideways across the seat like an over-size catch from the sea.

"Success! Bit of purchase, that's all I needed. God bless you. Oh, you're an angel all right, straight from heaven."

Janey rubbed her nose with her palm. She'd been called a few things in her time, but never ever an angel, not as far as she could remember.

"You had the common sense to come in, you clever girl. Did I kick up a terrible din?"

"Yeah! I didn't know what was up. I only come for jumble, then I heard you ..."

"You saved my bacon! There! Who says there isn't someone up above looking after us?"

Janey shrugged. It had been no more than a bit of luck, really. *The Lord helps those who help themselves*, was what Lou always said, and she'd never found out any different.

Oh God! Lou!

He'd be going bananas outside! She made a move for the door. He'd come storming in in a minute to find out what the hell she was up to.

"Gotta go," she said. "If you're all right, like. Only my dad'll start doing his nut."

"Of course you must. But hang on, lovie, half a mo'. I've got no jumble, given it all to the church. But you're a good little girl, and I want to reward you ..." The woman's voice had gone thick in her throat, and Janey recognised the sound of someone suddenly feeling all choked up. Her old nan had used to get like that sometimes, when anyone talked about Grandad. The woman looked about along the mantelpiece, over at the other chairs and the sideboard, high and low. "I know you didn't do it for the money, you did it out of kindness, but I'm going to give you a reward all the same, and I won't take no for an answer. A *good* reward, mind." She looked at Janey and nodded, emphasising how generous she was going to be. "If only I hadn't lost the run of my blessed purse." She went on looking, and just for a moment Janey did, too, under the big table, alongside chairs, on the window sill, just in case the thing was handy. But it wasn't. It wasn't in the room.

16

"Oh, *bother*! I can't drag all over now. See, I've put it down somewhere. You'll think I didn't mean it."

Janey shrugged as if it didn't matter: but it was a bit of bad luck, not finding it, because the old girl definitely did mean it, she could tell: and when she got outside and told Lou the job was off, a couple of notes to chuck him would have come in very handy: could well have saved her from a good shouting.

"Give us my walker, lovie." The old woman pointed to the lightweight walking frame. "I'll be right as rain in a bit, get around like one o'clock." Janey picked the frame up and set it by her chair. "Now you come back tomorrow and I shall have that purse, and you shall have a good reward. A *good* one. I mean that or my name's not Nora Woodcroft."

Janey believed her. But it really was a shame she couldn't find the thing now. She shrugged again, dropped her shoulder, started to go.

"You don't live far do you?" Nora Woodcroft looked her up and down. "Over the council estate...?"

Janey narrowed her eyes, scared she'd been recognised; said nothing.

"Never mind, dear, that doesn't make any difference to me. You come back tomorrow and you shall have it ..."

"All right."

"Good girl. Knock at the front."

"Yeah." Janey felt like doing a curtsey. The old girl was sitting up in her chair like a queen now, giving orders. It was funny how quick she'd changed from being in dead trouble down on the floor.

"By the way, what's your name? I ought to know what to call you, oughtn't I?"

"Kelly." It came quickly, without thinking.

"Kelly ... There's a lovely Irish name. A colleen, are you?"

"Dunno." Janey didn't know anything about that: it made her sound like a dog. But she did know you didn't give anything away to anyone, not when you were playing the

17

game Lou was, not even to old girls who made jokes about their knickers and promised you a reward.

"Anyway, you close that door tight. Go out the front way, and I'll expect you tomorrow afternoon. There's a love." Suddenly, the old woman looked tired. "I think I'm going to have five minutes ..."

Janey slid off round the door.

Nora Woodcroft smiled again. "Bye-bye, Kelly, love. And thank you, dear ..."

"It's O.K. See you." And with a tight smile of her own, Janey let herself out of the front and went to face up to Lou.

TWO

"You should've thrown the rug over 'er 'ead an' got on with it!"

Reggie Turner spat the words and baked beans over the settee: and although his eyes didn't flicker from the blood-bath on the video, Janey knew he meant what he said. That *was* what he would have done.

"Did she 'ave any good stuff?"

"Dunno. It wasn't posh. Sort of, ordinary. A ton of lead in one of her windows."

"You never let nothing go, do you?" Lou Turner came into the doorway with a can of beer to his mouth. "Stupid lead! We could 'ave cleaned out in there if you'd kept your wits about you. Place like that – them old girls don't know 'alf the value of what they've got . . ."

Janey wiped a trickle of tomato sauce from up her arm. Let them go on. What they didn't know was, she'd got a reward coming when she went back, a good one. Which'd probably leave more in her pocket to herself than she'd get from turning the place over with Lou.

"Now I'll be on the ear-'ole again for a drink tonight! I'd been saving that place up . . ." He crushed the can in his fist and threw it into the fireplace. "Little madam!" he suddenly shouted, and turned away to kick up the stairs to the bathroom.

Janey went on eating, deaf-eared. Let them get on with it! Spinning an empty place for a bit of silver was one thing, but leaving an old girl in a state while you got it done was something else. She shivered. "I'm cold. When we gonna 'ave the fire on?"

"We ain't." Reggie was still eye-deep in his horror.

"It's all right for you, you're goin' out!"

" 'Ard luck! You do your job proper an' y'can 'ave things."

19

"You wasn't there so you don't know!"

With a sudden twist, Reggie thrust his face into Janey's. "Shut up! I'm tryin' to watch suthing!"

Janey jerked her head back from the smell of his breath. She hated this kid, Lou's boy. Skin-head and hard just to be hard, and all mouth. Lou wasn't so bad: her mum's boy-friend she could handle, when they were on their own. But his toe-rag son, Reggie, was something else. Reggie was all sorts of *filth*.

"Tea! Mug 'o tea, you! An' shift yourself!"

Janey swore and went into the kitchen. Why couldn't her mum have taken her when she'd run off with a new bloke? Why leave her with Lou and this animal? For the millionth time she wondered if there wasn't something she could drop into the cup with Reggie's tea. What about getting some rat poison one day? That'd be just about right, she thought. No-one'd miss the vermin, that was for sure.

"Janey! Thought you said you couldn't come."

Mary Richards was in her bare feet. As she opened the door she wiped something secret from around her mouth and dusted the evidence off her hands: the thump of heavy music came out of the house from behind her like a big animal escaping.

"Come on in. She ain't gettin' back till ten. What time you got to go?"

"No special time." Janey shivered. When she'd had a good warm-up would be soon enough. " 'Fore she comes in, anyhow."

"O.K. We can try on her clothes." Putting on a shiver Mary looked really wicked with the thought of pushing her luck in her mother's bedroom.

Janey smiled. Poor old Mary, she'd die if she knew what Lou and her got up to. Mary's idea of breaking the law was robbing chocolates out of the cupboard or trying a bit of colour round her eyes. Doing something bad enough to get you sent away was right outside her mind.

20

"Got some Coke?"

"Yeah!"

They went through the house, past the loud front room and into the back kitchen. Janey liked it in the kitchen. She was used to front rooms, ate everything off a chair arm or a tin lid, all bent over on the settee. Front rooms were two bob for her. But a kitchen like this was really nice; people sat up at a counter on tall stools in here and had proper places for things in cupboards; and they cooked and ate and listened to Capital, and got on with things and talked. It was where they had a laugh, as well. She'd even gone home from here one night and tried to copy it at her house. Not the stools, she couldn't do that, but putting things in a bit of order – and all she'd got was a face from Lou for moving his fags and a mouthful of filth from Reggie for copying blacks. But the biggest put-down of all had come later: in bed, when, going over it all, she'd suddenly realised that it wasn't really Mary's kitchen she'd wanted to copy, not as such: it was Mary's family, and ever since her mum had run off there'd never been any chance of doing that.

"What happened with you, then? Finish early, robbing your bank?"

"Yeah, they was shut, and it's real hard work getting one of them machines to put up its hands." She already had it worked out, of course, liked to keep a bit of crooked talk going for Mary, who never knew what to believe and what not, but who always acted as if she secretly liked the mystery.

"So you ain't rollin' in it? Only I got an idea." Mary was suddenly being serious. "Was goin' to ask you, 'fore I definitely made up me mind."

It had gone all quiet. The tape in the stereo had stopped.

"What d'you reckon to this new Olympic Gymnastics Club down the Deptford Centre?"

"Eh? Never heard of it." And she hadn't. Janey was usually the last sort of person to hear about new things the kids were doing.

"It's some firm; you know, it ain't council, you have to pay.

But they got these Olympic people, you 'ave to pass tests and that to get in. An' you have to go regular, two, three times a week. It's real training, like, for top kids. Only trouble is, it ain't cheap."

Janey's face didn't change by a flicker. "You going?" she asked, in the voice she'd use choosing between first and second sittings at school dinners.

"Might. My mum wants me to. My dad says he don't mind. Thought I'd see what you reckoned . . ."

Janey looked at her, knocked back the rest of her Coke in one gulp: but that quick pain she felt inside was nothing to do with the gases. It was the sudden grab of jealousy. Olympic coaching in gymnastics! If there was one thing she could do in school, it was gymnastics. If there was one thing apart from being mates with Mary which made her feel good, it was running at boxes and somersaulting through the air; sort of being the boss of her body. But it was stupid even thinking about this. If it wasn't cheap then it wasn't for her. Nothing ever was. She stared at Mary's eyes because she knew them well, and what she saw in them now told her how that jealous pang wasn't only about gymnastics, either. It was about how she stood with Mary, too. Because Mary was really good at gymnastics, and Janey knew the signs all right. She might say she was waiting to know what Janey reckoned, but it was only her being nice. She'd go, she'd join – she'd have to. And you couldn't really fault her for that. The trouble was, things like this had happened before with other mates; they were always happening. People drifted away when she couldn't keep up, they joined things and left her behind when she couldn't go with them – fan clubs, dancing, pony riding. Not that all that stuff was much good to her, she'd hate the lot of it, but living on the dole and Lou's thieving meant she could never follow where they went – and they soon forgot boring old mates who didn't know a saddle from a sore bum.

The difference was, Olympic Gymnastics she did fancy; and she could definitely handle it, too. Imagine her and Mary being trained-up to go in big competitions. Fancy showing off something you could do instead of keeping something secret . . .

"I'll have to think about it." She supposed she could put Mary off for a bit, see how things went. If she couldn't raise the cash herself – and really, how could she? – there was always an outside chance Mary might change her mind.

"Let us know, then. Be good if you did come."

"Yeah!"

And then a new sort of silence seemed to draw itself between them, like prison visiting, one on the inside, one on the out. Janey cast around for some bright remark to make, something to take them back to where they'd been, but she couldn't think of anything to say at all: while Mary's disappointment at not having her idea jumped at was obvious as she sat down with a bump in a chair.

"Put another tape on."

"Yeah. O.K."

So they danced another tape through: but when it was over they both seemed relieved for Janey to go. They didn't go into Mrs Richards' bedroom, didn't try on her clothes. Instead, they said their ta-ra's, all their enthusiasm in their hands instead of on their faces, and Janey went off to wander through the estate, back to her tip of a kitchen and Reggie and Lou.

"You'll have a little drop of something in your tea, won't you, Nora? After what you went through yesterday?"

"Yes, I think I will, dear. Nice of you to ask."

Mrs Woodcroft got up slowly from her chair and steadied herself between its back and the small kitchen table. It took her a while, but then everything did these days. After a moment or two to be sure of her balance she gave all her attention to the distance between the chair back and the dresser, and with a determined set of her face, she launched herself across the open space, grabbing and gripping with shaking fingers at the edge of the work surface. It was narrow, not much of a grip, but she knew it like an old friend, the way she knew the inside jamb of every door, the handy corners of every piece of furniture. "Got you!" She relaxed, and one-handed found her medicinal brandy in a drawer, wrapped among the tea-towels. She slipped it in a pocket of her overall because she'd need two hands for the journey back, and after a sharp intake of breath for the courage to go, she made the push to get her back to the table.

"Thank you, dear, that was a nice idea." She poured a modest tea-spoon into her tea.

"No more than you deserve, young Nora."

Mrs Woodcroft looked across at her gallery of Kodak Samantha's and sighed. She was on her own. She often talked to herself in cheerful bursts, while she quietly wished Canada wasn't so blessed far away.

"Cheerio, Nora." She sipped at the cup like the wickedest drunkard around, her eyes closed to concentrate on the taste.

But there wasn't time to savour it. The bell above the door hummed for a split second then burst into a long, clear ring.

"Blow!" She drank the tea more vigorously so as not to waste the brandy. "Coming!" The cup would be cold by the time she got to the door and back.

Once she got going on her frame, she wasn't too bad. The first kick-off was always the worst, she told people – having to chance her arm on the lightweight thing without having a chair or a table to lean on, forcing her feet to move when they were stuck to the floor by the fear of falling. Going round the furniture was different to shuffling out on her own with only this aluminium thing to keep her steady. It was like anyone else going out on a tightrope.

"Come on, feet, come on, blow you!"

She got agitated. It was about now when the bell usually rang again. She shut her eyes and willed herself not to think of her feet as being ankle deep in sand. A ballroom, she was in instead, that sometimes worked, gliding in the long swoop of a tango as she'd once done with Alfred. One, two, three-four; da, da, da, one, two three-four; and all at once she was off on her frame, hands in front of her, head up; lift, shuffle, shuffle; lift, shuffle, shuffle; out into the hall. The long runner was gone, now it was flat parquet flooring all the way. "Coming, coming," she called, and she slow-danced her National Health partner to the front door.

It never crossed Nora's mind that one day there might be somebody there who wished her harm, a mugger or a con man: she'd avoided all that, somehow; only read about it, as if it could happen to other old people but never to her. So she opened the door when she got there without any spying or calling to find out who it was.

"Hello, love. I didn't go away, I could hear you coming on your contraption."

It was Miss Stephenson from the church, wrapped in the woollen cape she always wore and carrying a basket over her arm. To Nora she was always the spitting image of Little Red Riding Hood at fifty.

"A really grand day God's given us. Just a nip in the air to prepare us for what's to come ..."

And a nip in the tea to keep our peckers up, Nora thought. She pulled back on her frame to give Miss Stephenson room to come in, hoping against hope that she'd pushed the kitchen door shut on the sight of her secret bottle.

"Come in the front, Miss Stephenson," she said. "You're out and about bright and early; but it's nice to see you."

"And you, love, we do so miss you at our services. But I always think the good Lord knows," Miss Stephenson added. "He sees all."

Which is why I won't go to heaven! Nora thought. "I'm not sitting down because of getting up, but do make yourself comfy." That usually kept a visit like this on the short side.

But today it wasn't going to work. "I *want* you to sit down, love. I'll give you a hand up, never fear. I want to talk to you, Mrs Woodcroft." And Miss Stephenson clearly wasn't going to take no for an answer. She put her basket on the floor and with a swirl of her cape like a conjurer she sat herself down on the edge of a best armchair. The movement brought a fine sprinkling of soot from the chimney down onto the fanned paper in the grate.

"Oh?" As elegantly as she could, and a little bit heady now from the brandy, Nora lowered herself into the opposite chair, dropping the last six inches out of control and just managing not to say her usual 'Wallop!'

"I'm not going all round the houses, it is about your poorly walking that I've called," the church visitor went on, with Yorkshire straightforwardness. "You're not getting any younger, love, are you?"

Nora had to smile to herself. The cheek of it! Fancy having the nerve to come out with that, she thought. "None of us are, dear, are we?" She looked at the earnest face which would never have the benefit of a drop of under-eye cream or a touch of colour to help it. "What makes you say that?"

"The Reverend Timms, the Ladies' League, all of us. We're concerned about you, love. We're worried about you being on your own." She sat with her legs apart like a monk and leant forward, elbows on her knees. "I'll confess I sometimes lie awake in my bed worrying about you – having a tumble, not getting your food in, keeping cl . . . keeping like, everything as you want it."

Nora suddenly saw red. What was that? *She'd been going to say 'clean' – keeping clean!* The sauce of it, the damned cheek! Nora's eyes stared hard across the hearth, a real anger fuelled on the brandy. They could worry as much as they liked about her falling, or whether she ate enough, but to question her keeping clean! *Her!* They could inspect. They could bring a team of inspectors, go where they liked, look in all the drawers, go in any corner, behind anything – they could even take a look at what she'd got on underneath if they wanted to: to raise the question of her keeping clean was just too much!

She swallowed, knew her face was red. "I don't think you'll find I can't cope," she said, tartly. "The stairs are no trouble, I can get up and down those stairs like one o'clock, and I always

26

get my work done. It's only the garden I've let go, and I can soon get a man in. I'm perfectly capable, and perfectly happy, thank you, if you'd be good enough to inform the Reverend Timms and the Ladies League." Put that in your pipe and smoke it! she thought. She'd had this before from her daughter in Canada. *Why don't you go into an old person's flat? It'd put our minds at rest, knowing you're being looked after.* Well, she wouldn't. It was her *mind* that mattered, and that was young yet. She wasn't going to sit around all day with all those old fogies, not for anybody. It was just these damned legs that wouldn't always do as they were told, that was all – but they'd get better. She'd come into this house fifty years before as a young woman, and the day she left it would be the day they carted her out in a wooden box. No! She wasn't going to budge, and that was all there was to it!

"Nothing drastic, love, don't be alarmed. We were thinking, us at the church, about a little rota of people to come in and give an eye to you, that's all. Mrs Timms, Miss Rush and Mrs Pocknell, myself, of course, and there'd be bound to be other willing souls." Her voice dropped as she looked into Nora's eyes. "You're much loved, you know ..."

Nora still shuddered. Imagine that lot having the run of her house! Over my dead body, she wanted to say, much loved or not. "It's very kind of you all, Miss Stephenson. Give them all my thanks, won't you, but I can manage beautifully, thank you. If I want a Home Help I've only to apply, tell them, and if I want Meals on Wheels I'm entitled. So ..." And with the biggest effort of will she'd made for years, a do-or-die attempt to show the church helper how fit she was, Nora pulled herself up out of her chair, arms shaking but somehow all in one movement, and she grabbed at the frame by her side. "I won't come to the door with you, I'll just brush that soot up while I'm in here." Showing Miss Stephenson the struggle she'd have getting across this soft carpet was something she didn't intend to do.

"All right, love, but do remember the offer is there, won't

you? And don't you be too independent. I can still see a text from when I was a little girl. 'We that are strong ought to bear the infirmities of the weak.' Was it St. Paul who said that?"

"Very likely, dear. He was a wise old bird, wasn't he? But I'm a long way from being weak, thank you. I could knock mincemeat out of Miss Rush *and* Mrs Pocknell combined."

Nora laughed to ease the awkwardness of her retort, but she half-turned the top of her body towards the door, to let the other know she was expected to go now. She couldn't get rid of her quickly enough. She did hope she hadn't been too straight with her, she didn't like unpleasantness; in fact she'd go all round the houses not to offend anyone – but to have suggested she wasn't keeping herself clean: well, that was as bad as people not fancying your cooking.

With a sad smile at having failed, Miss Stephenson stood up and came towards her. But as quickly as it had come, the smile vanished. "Whatever have you done to your face, love? You've bruised your cheek." Miss Stephenson stepped back and tut-tutted. "Oh, you've had a tumble, haven't you? Don't try to pull the wool, love, you've had a tumble, I know you have."

Nora just stood there, she couldn't even trust her balance enough to put a hand to her face. She had the terrible, unworthy desire to lift the frame and bring it down with a wallop on Miss Busybody's brainbox: not to hurt her, of course, but to show her, make *her* look stupid. But instead, she had simply to stare back, speechless, like a naughty little girl who'd been found at the biscuits.

"Everyone only wants to do what's best for you." Miss Stephenson picked up her basket and creaked it out of the room. "And remember, *you're much loved*. You think on that." And with the quiet dignity of being firm on her feet, Miss Stephenson pulled the front door shut behind her.

"Where d'ya reckon you're goin', poncin' yourself up like a tart?"

Reggie leered round the bathroom door.

"Clear off! I'm in here!"

It hadn't had a lock on it since Janey's mother had busted it the night she went. Janey could only ever spare one eye for the smeary mirror.

"Goin' up West, are you, then?" His voice had the slime of a snail on it.

"Clear off, I said!"

"Huh!" Reggie choked back a wet laugh. "You look like somethin' off the cartoons!" He slammed the door so hard, it bounced open again.

Janey shut it with a foot and looked at herself in the mirror. She didn't look too bad, she reckoned. She'd given her face a good go, got in her ears, and she'd pinched a drop of Lou's shampoo to put a shine in her hair. No, she didn't look too bad at all. There wasn't a lot anyone could do with hair like hers, but when it had a wash it came up like her mother's, all curly, silky soft and black as pitch.

What to wear had been the hardest to decide. Janey wore all her clothes till they were so bad someone said something, the usual 'flea-bag' stuff, then she'd bundle them up in a couple of carriers, get some money off Lou and drag them round to the launderette. And that time was getting close, she was running really short; but by a stroke she'd gone into Lou's bedroom while he was down at the pub and found something left behind in the bottom of the wardrobe – a short black skirt too much out of the fashion for her mother to take. And now it fitted her a treat, being smaller. After that, washing out a tee-shirt in the kitchen sink had been easy, and though it was creased – the iron was locked in Reggie's room – it wouldn't look too bad if she tried to keep her arms folded.

She came out of the bathroom, and listened to Lou. You could hear people clearing their throats next-door-but-one in these thin-walled houses: and this Saturday morning half the estate must have heard Lou snoring. It was obvious he hadn't had too hard a time finding someone to buy him a skin-full. At least there wouldn't be any call on her for a while: she could

29

safely get lost for a couple of hours. Reggie had gone all quiet, up to something in his bedroom, so she'd just go when she was ready now. Get that reward. And if it turned out to be what she hoped it was, then it was straight down to Macdonalds for the biggest thing they did. She looked down at her skirt. Yes, the biggest king-size going, because there was tons of room for letting out the belt on this, and she hadn't had anything tasty for ages.

It seemed funny, going up to the old woman's house like a proper visitor. If the gate hadn't caught on the tiles she'd even have banged it behind her, just to make a noise. She walked briskly down the path and enjoyed not wasting her time looking at the ground-floor windows, searching for signs. She did stop and look at that huge stained-glass landing window; how could she go past that? Then it was boldly up to the front door and press her finger on the bell again. And this time she *could* read the name: it wasn't so faded when you knew what it said. *N. Woodcroft.*

The bell rang deep in the house. This morning – although Janey didn't feel the need to look and listen very hard – she saw the changing light in the crinkles, heard a couple of 'Coming's', until the shape of something moving in the passage gradually became the old lady. Like with the name, Janey thought, it was easy telling, when you knew what to expect.

The door swung open wide.

"Kelly!"

It was all Janey could do to stop herself looking behind her.

" 'Lo."

"Oh, you do look nice. Like a bandbox. What pretty hair."

Janey folded her arms across her creases and put her weight casually on one foot to make the action right. "Yeah?"

"Come in, lovie, don't stand there all shy. My goodness, you take me back a few years ..." Awkwardly, Nora Woodcroft inched back to let Janey step in. And the girl could see that she'd taken some trouble with her appearance, too. The blouse she wore didn't look cheap, and she had a beautiful brooch like a silver butterfly. The woman led the way out into the kitchen and sat herself down with a bump, waving at a chair for Janey to join her at the table.

"Do you like lemonade? Girls do still like lemonade, don't they? R. White's?"

"Yeah. Ta."

"Over there, in that cupboard: you can be my legs. You've got five minutes, haven't you?"

Janey nodded. She went to the low cupboard the old lady was pointing at and took out the lemonade, carefully pouring two smallish glasses. And following instructions, she found the biscuits in a big sweet tin called a barrel and carried it – with two plates from the dresser – back to the table.

They sipped and crunched together.

"My father, God bless him, used to roll up a little spill of paper and put it in our glasses, us girls, to take the bubbles out of the lemonade. He used to think the bubbles would make us too high-spirited." Nora Woodcroft suddenly laughed again, loudly. "Didn't work, I can tell you!"

Janey smiled and rubbed her nose with her palm. "My nan ..." She caught herself, and stopped.

"Yes, lovie, go on. What about your nan?"

"Oh, nothing." She'd been about to break the first rule Lou had drummed into her. *Don't trust anyone. Not anyone! Then you'll never give nothing away.* She listened instead.

"He used to break the bottles and get the stoppers out for us, the gob-stoppers, what we used for marbles. Only it made our mother cross because there'd be a ha'penny deposit on a lemonade bottle. And times were hard, I can tell you ..."

Janey saw the faraway look in the old lady's watery eyes, or was that a bit of a tear? Perhaps you *never* got used to your mother not being around, the girl thought, not even when you were an old age pensioner ...

"Wish they'd bring back deposits on things. One of these throw-it-away litre things and your pedal bin's full, isn't it?"

"Yeah." Janey supposed so. Only, their pedal bin was a

31

plastic carrier over by the back door: and when no-one fancied going out in the wet it turned into a soggy pile of muck. But you got used to it, like everything else, just stepped over it a bit higher.

"Which strikes me ... er ..." Nora Woodcroft looked embarrassed. "I don't suppose you'd run mine round to the dustbin for me, while you're here? They come on a Monday. I needn't go out the back any more then ..."

"Yeah, don't mind." Janey got up and went over to the sink. Do this and then she'd *have* to get given her reward, wouldn't she? And after that it was straight down to Macdonalds for her treat. She took a newspaper-lined pedal bin from behind a low curtain under the sink. "Where's your dustbin?" She'd missed seeing it the day before.

"Turn left, it's round by the gate." The old woman smiled. "Oh, you are a willing girl."

Janey opened the back door and looked out, saw what she hadn't had eyes for the day before: a long, overgrown garden where rotting apples still lay in the grass, hollowed out by birds and by insects: she saw the frame of a swing without a seat: took it all in now with the lingering gaze of someone who had permission to be there. Above her the sky was clear and bright, and she watched a heavy aeroplane in its final turn towards Heathrow, heading into a massive thundercloud which had risen up on the other side of London. But here, in the sun, looking out at the storm, she had a sudden, warm feeling of well-being. "It isn't half black over Bill's mother's," she said; and ran round the corner to empty the bin.

You can tell tons from what people sling out. That was something else Lou was always telling her. Look out for the cardboard packing from a video, and steer clear of places with dog food tins, that sort of thing. Janey flicked a professional eye over the old lady's rubbish as she dropped the kitchen scraps in. A few potato peelings poking out of a newspaper parcel, an empty tin of Silvo, a small fish fingers box and two broken cups. Hardly worth the dustmen coming. But Silvo told a story ... People

32

didn't have Silvo if they didn't have silver to clean, did they?

She replaced the lid and ran back to the kitchen.

"Do you know, lovie, I haven't heard that since my sister went ..."

The old woman's head was resting on her palm.

"Eh? What's that?" Janey cocked her head to listen. Was she on about the aeroplane, or some music somewhere?

"That old saying – 'black over Bill's mother's'. Where did you pick it up?"

Janey hesitated: then decided to risk it.

"My nan. Like, my dad's mum. My *old* dad's, not this one. She's dead now. Said it all the time when she saw a big cloud."

"Local, was she?"

Janey stared. "No, she was all there, same as you."

"I mean, she came from round here, did she?"

"Oh! Yes. Back of the town hall. She was always saying it. Same as that 'one o'clock' you said yesterday. Always saying that, she was."

Nora Woodcroft swayed like someone joining in one of the old songs. She clapped her hands. "That's right, the one o'clock gun, in the Arsenal. Set your clocks by it, you could. Dear-oh-lor, you don't hear those sayings any more, not with people dying off and moving away." Her face clouded over. "And what do you get instead? Swearing all over the place."

Janey nodded, as if she was disgusted by it, too. When all at once her hands were grabbed by the old woman and shaken up and down, like someone dancing with a baby.

"Oh, what a treat it is to have a real girl in the house instead of those bits of things on the television. You are an angel ..." And Janey was released so suddenly she nearly fell over. "Here, I've got something to show you. I bring it down for a clean, regular." Nora Woodcroft looked uncertain. "Don't think I'm showing off, will you, but it's just struck me you'd be the sort who might be interested. Now, what do you think of this?"

From inside a drawer, wrapped in a bright yellow duster,

33

she pulled out something about thirty centimetres long. It could have been a vase, or a goblet. She cradled it like a baby for a few moments before she tantalisingly began to unwrap its covering.

"Now, then: what about this?"

"Oh, yeah ..." Janey looked admiringly at what she'd revealed. It was a silver man, like a film award from Hollywood, only instead of being caught standing still this man was in a moving position.

"Valentino, doing the tango. 'Rudy', after the old film star. My Alfred and I, we won that in the All British Dancing Championships, years ago at the Lyceum. We used to teach, you know."

"Yeah?" This was what the Silvo was all about, then; it was gleaming. Worth a bit, Janey reckoned.

"Oh, and that was a night! Ballroom packed to the rafters, and, say it as shouldn't, the best from up and down the country in there." Her eyes were wide open but sightless as she looked back down the years. "There was one couple from Morecambe, George and Lily Henshaw, we thought they'd be bound to take it again. Very good, they were! But somehow, I don't know, they danced well enough, but everything we'd practised came off a treat, not a hesitation. And we'd worked out such a routine! A bit like those skaters do today, kept putting extra bits in to show off!" Nora laughed. "Made me puff and blow by the end, I can tell you! But we did it! When the marks came up, we'd won, and the whole place went mad!"

"Yeah?" Now Janey clapped her hands, for Nora.

"And we had to go up on the bandstand, and Alfred made a little speech; and here he is! Our Rudy!" Nora hugged the statuette. "Do you know, if it wasn't for my daughter I think I'd have him buried in with me when I go!" She held him to her chest and folded her hands across, winking an eye. "Just to remind the good Lord I wasn't always a cripple!"

"Go on! Get about a bit on that baby walker an' you'll be all right again, I bet."

Nora Woodcroft smiled at the encouragement and patted Janey's hand. "*It's all over my jealousy*," she suddenly sang in a high, clear voice: the first line of something vaguely familiar to Janey. "We won it with that," she said. "*Jealousy*. Often have that running through my silly old brain."

Janey shook her head. "It's not silly. I get stuck with tunes an' all. Everyone does ..."

"If only ... Oh, it's so nice to be near a bit of hope." Nora Woodcroft's eyes had gone watery again.

"I'll put him up here, eh?" Janey took the silver trophy. It was heavy too. If that was all silver it had to be worth a small fortune. "Did things better in those days, didn't they? I won a gymnastics medal at school. Looked all right, but let go of it an' it floated round the room!"

The old woman laughed. "Oh, you do me good, you really do. You really do!"

Janey leaned on the back of a chair, suddenly feeling relaxed. "My nan used to say I did her good," she said. "I used to go up her house after school for a few jobs: but we never got much done. She just used to like to talk. I s'pose you get a bit lonely ..."

"You can say that again!" said Nora.

"Yeah, good as a tonic, my nan said I was. Said she was gonna take me up the doctor's an' sell me by penny numbers in bottles of medicine."

The old woman stared at Janey and nodded her head. "I can see that ..."

"Once I ..." Now Janey wasn't caring, she was disobeying all Lou's rules, but somehow she felt she had to. "Once I went over to help her shift a telly upstairs for a party – 'cos she started doing silly things like that on her own if you didn't stop her – and we was halfway up the stairs, and I looked at her and she looked at me, and with the pull of that big telly we both had these daft looks on our faces ..."

Nora was beginning to sway and laugh, nodding as if she knew the experience of old.

"... An' we stood there and we couldn't move for laughing and we couldn't let go ... Nearly did ourselves a mischief! An' afterwards my nan said that laugh was better than all the party turned out!" Suddenly Janey felt herself going red, felt her lips wet with too much talking.

"I know that feeling." But Nora was leaning forward, joining in the mood, swapping a story on equal terms. "Alfred and I once moved a gas cooker across the kitchen. I swear I thought I'd hurt myself; not with the cooker, mind, with the laughing. Our faces were so ... comical!"

"They are, all taking-the-strain and serious!"

Nora put her head back and laughed again, a little bit false but to keep things going. "Tell you what ..." She pointed to the chair for Janey to sit down, poured them both another glass of lemonade. "Don't laugh, but I've just had the most stupid idea ..." She shut her mouth tight as if she didn't know how to begin: then, as if she were getting going on her feet she kicked herself off and the idea came spilling out. "Why don't you come round here now and then? Eh? After school, once or twice a week? Like you did for your nan? Come and do a few little errands for me – like that?" She waved at the pedal bin which Janey had left in the middle of the kitchen floor. "Fetch me a bit of shopping. Be my legs now mine won't work so well. What do you think of that ...?" She was smiling nervously as if what she'd said was enough to have her put away: as if having come out it sounded a crazy idea.

Janey stared at her. A job? Something regular? She'd really come here to get a reward, not a job ...

"I'm not short, it'll mean a nice little bit of pocket money for you. A bite of tea now and again. And a laugh – we both like a laugh, don't we? Watch your programmes if you like, be company for me ..."

"Dunno ..." It sounded better all the time, the tea and the telly, something to keep her out of Reggie's way. But it all sounded a bit too *organised*. And what about the days Lou suddenly decided she'd got to go with him?

36

"It'll do me a good turn, lovie. And stop a few tongues wagging, I can tell you. Not half. Listen . . . they'd all have me pushed off into a home if they could. Me! And it's only these stupid old feet of mine, won't get going when they're told. Why don't you ask your mum, see what she says?" The flushed face suddenly clouded over. "Tell her I don't want to rob her, though, if she needs you at home." Nora drew a fresh breath – and suddenly let it out, didn't use it. Her excitement had seemed to die in the air, like something a flame had burned up. "I'm a selfish old woman. I should've thought how you must be needed at home."

Janey dropped a shoulder. All she knew was she wanted to get away now with her reward, just in case she'd said too much.

"Only thinking of myself again! I swore I'd never get like that . . . " Nora switched on a false brightness. "Anyway, you came for your reward, Kelly, and you shall have it. Never let it be said I wasn't a woman of my word." From the pocket of her overall she took a small purse in pink felt, a simple thing with a plain stud catch and a rose embroidered in one corner. With a flourish she gave it to Janey. "Open it, lovie."

Janey did so. Folded inside was a smooth new ten pound note with edges sharp enough to cut a finger.

"Here, what's this?"

"It's no more than you deserve, Kelly dear; and if you're sensible you'll put it safe and sound in your post office book." The old woman's eyes searched Janey's face for some reaction. "And the purse is yours as well. I sat and ran that up last night. Gave me pleasure. Like my little rose, do you? More like a blessed cabbage you're saying . . . "

Janey crammed the note back into the purse and put it down the front of her tee-shirt.

"It's all right," she said. "Ta . . . "

"And you could just ask your mother if she couldn't spare you now and then, couldn't you? If you only come when you can . . . "

Janey smiled stiffly and turned to go: a slow turn with her mind working fast.

What if she did come here a bit regular? She could work it somehow, tell the odd lie, couldn't she? If the old lady threw money about like this all the time, she'd be stupid to say no. Janey got as far as the kitchen door; where she stopped, and sighed, and put a long-suffering look on her face.

"Tell you what," she said, "I'll give it a go. I'll come Monday, see what you need doing. If you like . . ."

"Will you?" The old woman clapped her hands like an infant at a party. "Will you? Oh, *good*. Good, good, good! You won't be sorry, lovie, you won't. I promise you."

Janey looked down at the floor.

"You've made a silly old woman very, very happy, do you know that? It's not looking so black over Bill's mother's now, I can tell you! Oh, lovely!"

Now Janey smiled. She couldn't help it. She couldn't think of any time she'd ever seen someone so happy over something, not since her nan had been alive. "Anyhow, I'll see you Monday," she said: and she went, shutting the door with a bang: while behind her the old woman sat at her table and blew her nose on a scented handkerchief.

"Well, would you believe it?" Nora shook her head. "Coming in here like that, a little rough diamond. It was all meant to be. How about another little drop of winkie to celebrate, Nora?"

"Do you know, I think I will, dear. What a lovely idea."

Nora had a little routine at bedtime. Being upstairs, she didn't need her walking frame because the banister rail ran the length of the landing and from that she could reach into every one of the rooms. It took her first to the bathroom where she did what she had to do with a sink and a bath and a low level cistern to support her. And there she undressed, too; left her clothes on the hot tank, and took her nightdress off it. Then, in her dressing gown, with her hair let down and suddenly looking

38

girlish, she went into Ruth's old room. It was kept ready for Sammy now, and Sammy had a nameplate on it from five years before, but it was really Ruth's room and it always would be. In there, on the dressing table, was a black-and-white photograph of her daughter, laughing in the sunshine of a grammar school afternoon. Nora couldn't easily get over to kiss the picture any more, but she always waved to it from the doorway, faced the direction she thought Canada was, and stood there to think a few thoughts before turning back for her own bedroom. And there, again, the routine was strict – but her illness had altered it slightly. Once it had been to kneel like an infant at the side of the bed and say her prayers for the family, for the queen and for peace on earth. Now she stood with one hand on the head-board, one over her brow, and prayed for Ruth and for Sammy and for those poor old legs of hers: please God let them start working again soon. Finally, and she was almost at the end of it by now, it was good night to Alfred. Wherever he was, whatever heaven meant – and she couldn't get away from the picture of some alpine island up in the sky – God bless Alfred and thank him for the good years they'd had together. And that meant holding and stroking and finally kissing Rudy, their silver statuette which stood in his place of honour on a tallboy behind the bedroom door, flanked by a silver-framed photograph of Alfred and the silk carnation he'd always worn on his evening dress. It was a sort of little shrine, always the last thing she saw before she went to sleep and the first thing she saw when she woke up: a reminder not only of all those years together, but of once being young and having a talent, and of accomplishing something with both.

Tonight, Nora said her brief prayer and unloosened her dressing gown before balancing back along the bed to the hook on the door. She wouldn't be sorry to lay down her bones tonight, she thought. And tomorrow was another day, wasn't it?

She reached for the door and steadied herself at the tallboy, taking smooth, cool Rudy into her hand. And while she stroked it, ran a forefinger over its smooth twenties hair, she told it what she'd done. It was the end of the day routine she'd had with Alfred, when something had needed to be said: just a few brief words to keep the other in the picture before tiredness called a halt.

"I hope I've done the right thing," she said. "I'm sure I have – but I've really thrown my hat over the windmill this time!" She laughed mysteriously. " 'What's all this?' you're saying, 'What's my Nora done now?' Well, I'll tell you: I've taken to a dear little girl, silly old fool that I am! Aren't I daft? She's not too special with her clothes, misses a few of the corners washing, but she's the genuine article: someone with a bit of go, a bit of sparkle . . . " Nora stopped and put Rudy down, looked him in the eye. "She's someone a bit like a girl I used to know, if you want it out, long before Alfred met me. Ordinary home, not much money to play with . . . " Her eyes glazed over as her mind went back nearly sixty years to her own poor childhood in Sutcliffe Road, to a mother who'd taken in washing and a father who'd worked in the Arsenal by day and waited at functions by night: to a time when, as a girl, she'd run round barefoot, and shown willing, and had appreciated someone giving her a little bit of independence.

"So don't worry, it'll work. Anyway, I've always been a good judge of character, prided myself on it." She laughed again. "Picked Alfred, didn't I?" And with that hint of defiance to cover the chance she knew she was taking, she kissed her husband's picture and put herself to bed: where, against all the odds, she slept without creasing the sheets.

THREE

"Sammy, are you going to eat these cookies or aren't you?"

"O.K., they're not planning to *walk away*, are they?"

"I want to get cleaned up before I go to town."

"So I'll eat them. Two cookies can't be exactly a garbage problem."

"No-one said they were. Just use a plate, huh? I can do without a load of crumbs."

"I'll go eat them in the shower if you like ..."

"Don't be so fresh. There's no need to be fresh." Ruth Seymore sighed and put the cookies in the Frigidaire, complaining to herself in a low voice about Canadian kids and mess and people who always had all the answers. Finally, in case John got back before her, she checked round the kitchen to make sure she'd left it in order, and she went to the key rack for her car keys.

She hadn't got to the car, though, when the mailman came – early for a change – and with one hand on the up-and-over, she had to stop and open the Air Mail letter from England right there because this one wasn't in her mother's old-fashioned loops. Always, at times like this, her heart seemed to miss a few beats, even though she knew she'd hear anything serious by telephone first.

But this was serious enough. Her trip into town suddenly became of very little importance. She ran into the house and tapped out a series of numbers on the telephone.

"John?" she said, almost before the connection was made. "Don't think I'm crazy, John – but you're going to have to cancel the fall vacation. See what you can get back on it. Only do it today, because I've just had a letter from England, from Mother's church." She'd held out, but now she started to cry.

"She's had a fall and they say she can't cope too well. I'll just have to take Sammy and go sort something out ..."

Sitting on the stairs listening, Sammy tried in vain to stop the smile from coming on her face.

"No, not when's school's out. Soon. Sammy'll have to miss a few weeks. Sure, I know you can't. Sure. But it's got to be this year, John, not next. It sounds ... real urgent ..."

And Sammy, who could just about remember her grand-mother from when she'd come over three years before, who signed photographs and cards with kisses and hearts to someone she never thought about, started to hug her knees at the joy of seeing the faces of all the kids who'd sell their mothers to swap places with her and take a trip to England in term time.

"'S just your 'ard luck, Turner!"

Reggie stood a metre from the Kawasaki admiring its trumpet exhausts, polishing the chrome with his eyes. It seemed to take a few seconds for the words to sink in.

"Eh?"

"I said, ''Ard luck!' If you ain't got the bread then I can't 'elp you ..." Spiros Kiperanous stood lounging in the doorway of his father's kebab house; not serving tonight, but at home to a special circle of friends. "You said you'd put down fifty an' you ain't come up with it. What you expect me to do, give you a savings card?"

If Janey could have seen the look passing over Reggie's eyes she could have told Spiros how close he came to a butt in the face. But Reggie held on. He kept his attention on the dual exhausts as if doing so could somehow keep the machine there for him.

"You said I 'ad first shout. You give me your word."

"Listen, son, you said you 'ad fifty quid. You give me *your* word. An' I said first one with fifty quid 'ad first shout. What you think I am, the Woolwich Equitable? You said you'd bring

42

it tonight, an' you ain't. That ain't gonna help me get my new one, is it? I got to put down a hundred. Be fair ..."

Boxer fashion, Reggie took in a deep breath through his nose, his fists seeming to be easing the stiffness out of a pair of new gloves. He moved his eyes slowly from the machine and onto the Greek. But it was wasted on Spiros. His father was there, and his brothers: he was on home territory.

"You can't fault me for showing it to Derry."

There was still a lot of breathing in and out.

"All right. All right, Kipper. But if 'e ain't got the bread then you get back to me, right? 'Cos I'm gonna get it real quick."

"I'll see what 'e comes up with. You prob'ly got a couple of days. But I don't owe you nothin', Turner. An' I tell you, son, you don't frighten me, neither, hard man or not ..."

Reggie really stared at him now. A chance of a pair of cheap wheels or a lesson for Kipper? It looked really touch and go for a few seconds. But at last Reggie managed a costly smile. "Don't be like that, Spire," he said. "No need for that sort o' talk, mate. I'll soon 'ave that cash an' we can shake on it. I ain't gonna let you down, you see ..."

Janey hadn't got far from Nora Woodcroft's, cutting through to the shopping centre, when the juices which were starting to work for Macdonalds began giving way to a different sort of feeling inside. It was all to do with what she'd been given: the size of that reward. Macdonalds was O.K., she started to think, a real nice treat if you had a quid or so to spend, but that old lady had given her a big one, a tenner – and wouldn't that go a fair way to getting her what else it was she wanted? What about Mary and the Deptford Centre? Wouldn't ten pounds be enough to get her a start in that? It was a fair amount. And what about the helping after school? Wouldn't that pay the subs? Then she'd have both, wouldn't she? A bit of gymnastics, but more than that, she'd run less risk of saying goodbye to Mary as a mate. Wouldn't that do her a better turn than a quick Macdonalds? Was it really worth breaking into a big note for a meal when keeping the money in one piece could buy her all that much more? And she had to face it, she'd probably have forgotten what she'd had by the time she got home.

It made a lot of sense. Suddenly she'd decided, and instead of walking slower and slower she turned straight round and went back the way she'd come, turning her mind off the food to thoughts of where she could hide the money from those two indoors: thinking up some place where she could safely put the tenner, together with any other bits of cash she'd get for helping the old lady. Which wasn't easy, finding a place. In a house full of thieves with no-one trusting anyone else, good hiding places were like gold-dust. If she even took a book indoors Reggie would grab it and shake it for what was tucked in the pages: all the bedroom floorboards creaked because they got lifted when anyone was out: and the bath panel hadn't had any screws since Janey was an infant. So where the hell would this ten pounds go?

She couldn't tell where the idea suddenly came from: perhaps it was seeing inside the old lady's cupboard that morning: but she smiled when it hit her, she even said "Got it!" out loud to a cat. Because she'd just thought of a place where Lou and Reggie would never look, not in a month of Sundays. What about in the Horlicks jar under the powder? Horlicks was something none of them ever drank, but then no-one ever threw the stuff away, either. It was one of those everlasting things some people had in the food cupboard, like packets of cake-mix. And that jar had been in there *years*. Her mum had bought it when Janey had fancied the taste of it once at her nan's, but somehow had never made it the same. Which was just the ticket: something which had hung about for ages and no-one gave a second look to.

It was really handy, sometimes, learning a crook's way of thinking. Being bent was a bit like being clever – except you never passed any exams in it.

While she walked, faster now she'd solved her problem,

44

Janey took the ten pound note out of the home-made purse and folded it up small, creasing the edges with her nails to help it stay flat under the powder, because she knew it had to be all ready before she walked indoors: once she got there, she'd have to move like greased lightning. In a house without a lock on even the bathroom door, there was never any safe time for secrets.

Another of the troubles was, from the outside of the house you could never be sure whether Reggie was in or out. He didn't have a car or a motor-bike to leave standing by the kerb, and with the curtains drawn most of the time the windows gave nothing away. Lou was no danger, Janey reckoned. He'd still be sleeping off the night before: laying down his eyeballs, as he called it. But it was Reggie. He'd come at you like a rat out of rubbish sometimes: there was just no telling with him.

As quietly as if she were going into a house on a job, Janey slid herself indoors: and like standing in a stranger's hallway, she stopped to listen for any sound from upstairs before moving. But all she could hear were the same old drunken snores from Lou; and not a creak from Reggie's room. She didn't move just yet, though. She always gave it longer than was needed. Patience, in the break-in game, was often the difference between winning and losing. Like Lou always told her: *you never THINK it's all right: you MAKE DEAD SURE.* Only when she couldn't hold it any longer did she ease her muscles out of the statue and quietly tiptoe into the kitchen. Carefully, without scraping it, she lifted a stool over to the wall cupboard and started moving jars and dusty tins to find what she was after. And there it was, right at the back where it didn't have to get shifted around any more: the Horlicks, half a jar of dark and lumpy powder behind a faded label. Staying balanced on the stool, Janey tried to unscrew the top. Strewth! Why did people have to do things up like they were never meant to come off? She gripped and she strained and she twisted: and in the end it gave, but only because she knew she had to make it. Things did, when it was down to you or do without. You only give up, she'd found out, when there's someone else to sort things for you.

With the top off, the stale Horlicks still had enough of its old smell to take her straight back to her nan's: but she didn't dwell on that, because that was another sort of strength you got, not dwelling on things. The stuff itself had gone very lumpy, but no problem: it was still deep enough to bury the tenner. Plus, being Horlicks, it wouldn't stain the money like cocoa would.

Janey took out the folded note and tried to bury it in the powder. It wasn't easy. Her fingers weren't quite long enough to make a decent hole, while her whole hand was too big to go in. She shook the jar and tipped; and finally she dropped the tenner in and covered it somehow in jumps and jerks like throwing dice. Now all she had to do was put the lid on and slide the jar back where it had come from in the dark of the food cupboard. Thank God for that! she thought. Things had gone right for once.

Some hope! It took Reggie five seconds to crash in through the front door and get to her in the kitchen. There wasn't any warning. There never was. In his big boots and frustration at losing a round to Spiros Kiperanous, it was bang, slam, rattle, and suddenly there he was staring up at Janey with an extra dose of hate all over his face.

"What the 'ell you doin' poncin' about up there?"

He was frowning and suspicious and he wasn't going to go away. Janey looked down at the ugly bones his skin-head showed, his pale and pimply indoor skin and the black holes of his face: eyes, nostrils, gaping mouth. What sort of a rotten life was it when you had to live with someone you hated?

"I'm gettin' this." She gave him a quick look at the Horlicks jar, desperately hoping the tenner in it still didn't show.

" 'Orlicks? Wha' for?"

He still wasn't moving, was going to see this through. He knew she was up to something, she could tell by his face.

"What do you think for, stupid? To have a drink, o' course!"

He started swaying, the old aggro sign.

"That's for night time. Y' don't drink 'Orlicks in the stupid day . . ."

"I do."

"Yeah?" Suddenly, he stopped swaying. "Lyin' cow!" His boot shot out and kicked the stool from under her. Janey screamed, grabbed for the cupboard but missed and fell in a tangle of hard stool-legs onto the floor. Her spine, her elbow, her neck – the pain went up through her body and made her yell.

She swore at him from down in the debris as the Horlicks jar ran all the way along the table and tumbled over to fall next to her on the tiles. Janey watched it go, saw it shatter in a sort of slow motion: saw the lumpy powder spill out, the broken jar rock backwards and forwards with the dead give-away of the ten pound note sliding slowly down an angle of broken glass.

"Oh, yeah? Gettin' a drink? 'Spensive taste you got! Where d'you get this, you little liar?"

"Here, what's that – in the Horlicks!" It was a pathetic attempt, and she knew it.

"Come off it! I ain't stupid!" He unfolded the bank note and stared at it, his hand white-tight so she shouldn't snatch it from him. "Where d'you get hold o' this?"

"Found it. Up there in that cupboard . . . "

"Yeah?" Without warning his free hand grabbed at Janey, into the belt holding up her mother's too-big skirt, and out came the new felt purse, screwed up in his nail-bitten fingers. "An' where was this – in a tea bag?"

"Give it back!" Janey kicked at him, grabbed at the stool. "You give it back, that's mine!" But he was stronger than she was, and he didn't even have to hurt her much to push her back to the floor. She was lucky, because now his mind was on something other than taking his frustration out on her. He was looking at the money, looking up at other jars as if it were only a part of what he could get: as if he knew there were secrets here – and he wanted in on them. "Now let's 'ave the truth!" He shoved the money in his back pocket and started to slide the belt from round the top of his jeans.

Janey tried a piercing scream, but it came out like one of those muted shrieks in a dream.

47

"All right, you pig, leave off! What you want to know?"

Reggie stopped his fiddling with the belt. "Where you got it, that's what I wanna know. You don't come by ten quids too easy."

"Found it. I did find it, that's the honest truth, but not up there. You can go through all the lot. It was the shops. I found it outside Patel's. Some old girl must've dropped it."

"Yeah?" He started swaying again, his mouth going the way which said he still didn't believe her. "That what you got all done up for, was it, goin' down the shops?"

"No . . ." But Janey couldn't think of another lie to tell him. There was no quick excuse, no saved-up line about robbing a bank to come to her rescue like it might have done with Mary.

He went for the belt again. "I said the truth, din' I? I tell you, you give it me straight or you'll 'ave this in a minute just for the 'ell of it!"

Janey looked up at him, saw that look still in his eyes. He meant it, the vicious yob.

"Yesterday, that house . . ." Janey started to sob because she knew she was beaten now, all ways. She knew he *would* use the belt while Lou was out cold and couldn't stop him. "An old girl give it me. For helping . . ."

"Yeah?" She watched Reggie do the nearest thing he could to smiling. "That's 'andy, then. Got plenty of these tucked away, 'as she?"

Janey took the half chance to get up. "Didn't see, did I? She only give me the one, honest. I didn't see her purse. But I'm going back, I can find out . . ."

Reggie took the note out again, looked at it, turned it over, ran his fingers over its smooth newness, flicked an edge with a fingernail. "Gets 'er pension put by, puts it all in envelopes, gas, electric, telly, I know the touch."

She bet he knew it, too, from when he went mugging in the Sheltered Homes. And it all sounded very likely, it was the way old people did it – the sort of thing Lou was on the look-out for all the time.

48

Already Reggie was tapping the note in what passed for thinking. "Listen, you go back an' you get 'old of the rest 'o this, you hear? Find them envelopes, turn 'er inside out! I got suthin' special to do with two or three more o' these."

"Yeah?" A sudden new interest whipped into Janey's face. She knew when to stand and fight and when to run. Her voice went all enthusiastic. "Give us a share an' I'll have a real good look next time."

"See what you get first." But now the belt was forgotten. "Today, it's got to be. Tonight. You get back quick an' do the business an' I could 'ave what I'm after by tomorrow!"

"Don't forget I want something for me, Reggie! If I go back it ain't all for you ..."

"We'll 'ave to see. But get in quick – you hear?"

Janey put on a whine. "Monday. I can't go till Monday. That's only two days. Else she'll smell a rat. It'll be easy Monday when she's showin' me round the jobs ..."

Reggie thought about it. "All right. Monday, then. But definite!"

He thrust his face at her, something cruel in his eyes. But he pulled away, went for the fridge instead and downed half a pint of milk. Then he slammed out of the kitchen with a loud burp and a sneering, satisfied grin on his face.

Janey's bed was the lumpiest in the house and her pillow was an old cushion stuffed with rolled-up tights. But most nights nothing kept her awake: she fell asleep quickly because she was exhausted. Lou's comings and goings and Reggie's music soon faded because the power to hear them had run out inside her head. She might have a short think about something that had happened in the day, hardly ever about tomorrow; then, like someone going under for an operation she'd slide steeply into a deep and dreamless sleep.

Tonight was different, though. Tonight, as hard as she tried, she couldn't sleep: and that was because she knew she'd tried to lie to Reggie for more than one reason. Definitely, she'd wanted to keep her precious ten pounds for herself; and definitely, she'd have done anything to stop being hit by Reggie's belt. But it was something else keeping her twisting and turning on her uncomfortable mattress – and that was the rotten way she felt about Reggie being in on anything to do with the old lady. To save her own skin, she'd sort of turned her over to him. And she didn't know why, but after talking to her, having a laugh, that didn't seem right. What she was planning with Reggie didn't seem like going on an ordinary job any more, not with her going back and doing it while she was pretending to be a help, playing on the old girl's soft heart. Somehow that seemed well out of line.

It was very late, one o'clock, could have been two, before Janey's head found some sort of peace between two mounds in her cushion and her over-tired brain eventually allowed her to sleep. But when the sounds of a quarrel next door woke her up, she knew there was something urgent she had to do, something she had to find out. While Reggie and Lou still slept, she got up, dressed and ran out of the house.

Her morning was Mary's afternoon and Janey found her washing-up when she rang the bell at two o'clock.

"Come in, come in, treasure," Mary's mother flapped her tea towel like a flag along the passage. "Good to see you, girl. Mary, look who's comin' to see you." It was almost better going to the house when Mrs Richards was in: she sometimes seemed more pleased to see her than Mary did.

"Come in, young lady, don't stand there bein' shy." Mr Richards was a small unsmiling man with a voice that was big and warm and kind. It didn't go with him at all. He was doing up his Underground jacket and straightening his legs. "Give this girl a glass of fizz, she looks like she's been runnin' all day."

Mary left the sink and poured some Coke; Mrs Richards flopped in a chair and watched them drink; Mr Richards said goodbye and went to work without his watch.

"Well now, you girls want private talk, I'm going for me lay down." Mrs Richards pulled herself out of the chair. "Just keep a clamp on your noise or I be back to visit you." She said it more as a laugh than a threat and went creaking off up the stairs.

Ignoring the hunger which the left-over plate brought on, Janey came straight to the point.

"This club, this Deptford Centre Gymnastics. How much d'you reckon it's going to cost? Mary?"

Mary was flipping the pages of her father's Sunday paper, searching for the bits he didn't let her see.

"Mary! I run all the way to ask you something."

Mary put the paper down. She had heard. "I got it writ down somewhere, got my mum to find out all the arrangements, like." She started rummaging.

"Just rough'll do. Only I want to know, see if it's, like, reasonable . . ."

"Here you are. I got it here." She squinted at the paper, although her eyes were good. "You have to pay a term's fees in advance, that's for the instruction, right: Fifteen pounds for a twelve week course and you've got to get the regulation gear to wear. It says."

"An' how much is that?"

True to form, Janey thought, old Mary really had got it sorted.

"Well, o' course, I got me leotard: pay what you like for them, three or four quid down the sports shop; then it's the proper club badge for your tracksuit – I dunno what that is, they don't say here – and the Award money, you know, for your badges, like, when you do the stages. And a quid to do the test."

"The test? What test?"

Mary snorted. "Well, they ain't takin' *anyone*, Janey. That's the whole thing. You've got to be stage one 'fore they'll even look at you. It's a proper thing. I'm doin' my test Wednesday . . ."

Janey pulled a face. "Test won't be no bother." She did some sums on the ceiling. "But we're talking about twenty quid just for gettin' in, plus the tracksuit."

"Something like that."

"Yeah, well . . . "

"So what you gonna do? You gonna join, Janey? Be brilliant, eh? You know, I thought you wasn't, the other night . . . "

"No. I want to. But, see, it's a lot of money, all at once." In a way, though, she knew it wasn't. It might have seemed that way yesterday, but that was before Reggie had twisted her arm.

"Go on. Con your dad. You ought to. Con someone, eh? You're brilliant at gymnastics. Come down with me Wednesday, we'll join together. What time you be here?"

A sudden thumping on the floor above made both girls jump. Mary's sudden burst of enthusiasm had got too loud.

"I might do," Janey whispered. "I've got a bit of working out to do. I'll tell you tomorrow if I can . . . " She looked at Mary's face all keen and she desperately wanted to join. But why couldn't it have been out of the question?

In a muffle of tiptoes and whispers Mary let her out, and after a quiet goodbye Janey walked slowly to the end of the street. She stood there and looked around: down one row of houses and then down another. What a state to be in! The long way back home would take her twenty minutes: the quick way more like ten, going past the old lady's house. And that was her problem, part of what her restless night had been about and her quick run down to Mary's: why she'd had to sort out where she stood by talking hard cash. After a minute or so, to the sound of a pub turning out, she suddenly chose the longer walk.

Because she'd just made up her mind what she was going to do. She was going to put herself first. She'd found out what, in a crazy way, she'd hoped she wouldn't: that the gymnastics could be well within her reach. She'd found out that she didn't need to con Reggie out of all that much to make her own life a bit nicer. And didn't that come first? Which meant she'd just found out, too, that she was going to do that business for Reggie, sleep well or not. But that didn't mean she fancied seeing any more than she had to of a kind old lady's house she'd definitely decided to rob.

FOUR

Janey told herself all sorts of things on the way to Nora
Woodcroft's the following Monday. Every step in the lorry-
cracked pavement seemed to throw up some fresh excuse for
what she was going to do: which was something new to her,
because usually she couldn't care less about the whys and
wherefores of the things she did.

Well, first of all, as she was always telling herself, you had to
look after number one in this life. If you didn't look after
yourself, who the hell else was going to do it? Which meant, if
someone had plenty of something and you needed a bit of it you
were quite in order to take it. Wasn't that what Robin Hood
was all about? Robbing the rich to help the poor? Well why
shouldn't the poor do it for themselves? She kicked at the kerb
with a broken shoe. And was anyone around here much worse
off than Janey Pearce?

Then what about, '*The Lord helps him who helps himself*'?
That's what Lou was always going on about: so much, it was a
wonder he didn't have it carved on the back of his bed. But it
was true, wasn't it? It was all about survival-of-the-fittest
round here. And what's more, if you didn't want to go under,
you didn't have to be too soft about who you turned over to stay
on top.

Then what about the old lady? You could feel sorry, but look
at that great big house! Bigger than her nan's had been. Look at
the size of it just for her. She'd be better off all round, miles
better off, in something small and on one floor with people
about. If she went in a flat – if she was forced to because some of
her money got pinched and people put the pressure on – well,
that'd almost be doing her a favour, wouldn't it? She wouldn't
see it, of course, but she could be thanking Janey for forcing it,

53

in the long run. She had some family somewhere, you could tell that from all the pictures, but where were they, leaving her to fall over on her own? It'd be a double good turn, forcing them to come and see she got looked after properly.

Janey began to walk a bit faster, pushed on by her excuses. But above all, she told herself, there was her own good to think about, what she'd get from her having the odd twenty quid – Olympic gymnastics and keeping in with Mary. Being good at gym gave her a real lift, and having a mate like old Mary was great: which made them just about the only two things in her life worth having these days. If she only knew, if she knew how she hadn't got a mum any more, wouldn't the old lady *want* her to have the money she needed?

The walk almost became a skip, the step of someone who'd talked herself out of any doubts about where she was going. Because last of all there was Reggie to think about. Giving him something to be pleased at, getting him off her back for a while couldn't be bad. And he'd be out of the house a hell of a lot more showing off round the district if he got that motor bike he was after.

Janey's skip became a run. She *had* to get the money, she told herself. There was no question about it.

She was there before she knew it, missed the house and had to backtrack because the place looked different somehow: it was smaller than she remembered; and the coloured glass in the window made her stop and look, showed up much more than the strips of lead now the sun was on it. And the rest of the place, too, looked different closer up. The front path had had a sweep, and the curtains looked as though they'd been given a shake and a straighten.

Janey rang the bell, leant against the porch, and suddenly started breathing hard. She knew all about waiting at doors but this was something different – coming over all nervous at the push of a button. This sort of jitters was something new: their old 'Have you got any jumble?' routine never had her stomach going over the way it was somersaulting right now. She knew what it was, of course: she needn't have been surprised. It was *knowing* the old girl that was turning her inside out.

But now there were changes in the light through the glass again and the sound of slow steps along the hall. "Coming! Coming!" Nora called.

With a toss of her black curls Janey tried to shake her doubts out of her mind. The door opened wide.

"Kelly, dear! You came! I knew you would, I knew you would!" The old woman leant against the wall and clapped her hands, smiling like an Away-Day advert.

" 'Course." Janey smiled too: but she couldn't get her heart into it.

"Enter!" Still leaning, Nora Woodcroft made a shaky gesture. "You can come round the back next time, none of this standing on ceremony. But today, it's the grand entrance. Now, what do you say to a cup of tea?"

"Yeah, lovely."

"And a chocolate biscuit. Let's be wicked, eh?"

Slowly, at the old woman's pace, Janey followed Nora down the hall and into the kitchen, where the small table was already set with a crisp, clean cloth and chocolate biscuits were sloping neatly on a plate.

"Have what you want, lovie, don't make a fool of your mouth. I do like to see a good appetite."

Janey sat with an elbow on the cloth and politely pecked at a biscuit. But it was hard to swallow down: that twisting inside was spoiling her appetite. From across the table she stared at one of the cardboard school photographs, face down on Nora's cushion. Meanwhile, the old woman steadied herself on the dresser, reached out for the back of the chair, and with a tense, determined look launched herself across the gap. "Now then," she said calmly, as if nothing had happened. "See what I've got down to show you."

She picked up the picture; and while Janey ate one biscuit, then two, Nora told her about the girl who was smiling out at them.

"Samantha," she said proudly, "my Canadian grand-daughter."

So that's where she came from. Janey thought she hadn't see her about the district. She looked a right snob, too, all teeth braces shining and so clean she had to have one layer less skin. And you could tell from the eyes she was the sort of kid who wouldn't hold your hand in Country Dancing, just grab your wrist or hang her fingers close and pretend for the teacher.

"Oh, she looks nice," she lied.

"And she is nice, Kelly, and she is nice. She writes me a lovely letter at Christmas, all newsy about her friends and her little ways. But that's never enough, is it? If only she was nearer. I do miss seeing her growing up."

"Yeah." Janey knew a woman who'd missed seeing someone grow up: her own mother.

"I thought you'd like to see it, knew you'd be interested. Now, that cup of tea."

Janey poured it. She was getting impatient. She'd better start doing some jobs, a bit of earning, she thought, or the old girl wouldn't have any reason to go for her purse; and then she'd never know where she kept her money things.

"You want me to get you some shopping?"

"Later, dear; later in the week. See, I'm all right for a bit. Don't mind what they say, I'm not totally helpless. But I tell you what you can do to help. You can wash these bits and put a mop across the floor for me. How about that? That'd do me a really good turn and you'll feel you've started, won't you?"

"Yeah, O.K."

"I'll get right out of your way into the other room. You'll soon see where these things go."

"Yeah. Course. Where's your mop?"

"Mop cupboard, by the back door."

Janey looked, as casually as she could. "O.K." What a stroke! She couldn't have wanted it better, coming so soon. A really good chance to be on her own and go over the kitchen! She might even find what she wanted and get away really quick. She had to face it, it wasn't going to be nice, doing what she had to: so the sooner she did it and got out, the better. Eh?

But the old girl would hang about. Janey started to think she was never going to go. She hovered on her frame in the doorway and kept finding last minute things to say; nothing important, a couple of stories, and all for the company, really. So the washing-up went very slowly because Janey needed to have things left to do when she was in there on her own. In the end she had to say something.

"I'm not gonna be much help to you if you stay on your feet all the time. You go and sit down. I'll give you a shout when I'm done."

"Quite right, Kelly, quite right." Nora Woodcroft laughed. "You tick me off. And don't they always say a kitchen's never big enough for two women?"

Janey shrugged. "I don't know about that." She'd never had that problem. But the old woman went and she shut the door behind her. And it had hardly clicked before Janey's on-the-job training from Lou started to go methodically into action.

First she slid the kitchen table across in front of the door and put the chairs on top of it, made a barricade. Well, you had to clear the decks to mop the floor, didn't you? She ran a tap to make a noise, both a good cover and something to make her sound really busy. Next she found the mop and bucket and put them handy so that she had something to turn to if she was forced to open the door. Then, quickly and expertly, she went through the obvious places where money things might be. *It's usually just where you reckon to find it*, Lou always said. *Nothing clever. Never credit people with being too clever.* So one of the kitchen drawers had to be favourite: experience told her that everyone had a place where reading glasses went, and letters, and rent books. And that's where wallets and purses usually went, too.

Tiptoeing to the dresser while the water splashed, Janey eased one of the dresser drawers open – slowly, pulling with a steady pressure, picking the one with the shinier handle – and good enough, it looked like the drawer she was after. Best gloves, a door key, Building Society books and a purse. Envelopes of money could be anywhere in there.

As if she could hear Lou talking her through it, Janey made sure she took only one thing out at a time, putting it back before she went for another. If what she was after wasn't here, the last thing she wanted was the old girl knowing she'd been having a poke around.

Purse first, then; a big plastic one, the sort old people can get their fingers in. Smothering its click in her cardigan, she opened it. A pound coin, some silver and a few coppers in the big compartment, a five pound note folded small in the next. Quickly, Janey lifted the buttoned-down compartment at the front. Nothing. Well, a book of postage stamps, that was all.

She swore to herself, disappointed. That hadn't been much. The rest had to be somewhere then. She put it all back, the fiver as well. Why spoil it all for five pounds? she thought. She turned away and ran the mop under the tap, wiped a quick swathe of water over the floor to look busy, and gave herself back to the drawer.

The Building Society books came next. Three of them, all named after different places. Janey looked at them closely. Going by the last numbers down the right hand sides she wasn't all that well off, the old girl. Hundreds and tens, not thousands and hundreds. So perhaps she had it in the bank or the post office. In which case where was her book? Janey went for the gloves next. What about them? If she was acting clever the old girl might have tucked her money up into them: just the sort of stunt an old girl would think of. Working faster now, Janey put the Building Society books back where she'd found them, carefully, in the right order, and she reached her hand in for the first rolled-up bundle of gloves.

"Are you looking for something, dear?"

By some great act of will Janey forced herself not to spin round and look guilty. But it was touch and go, and her hands had to grip at the dresser. How the devil had the old girl got back into the room through the table and chairs? And without making a sound? She'd swear nothing had moved. As calmly as she could, Janey turned away from the dresser drawer, smiling like someone caught doing a secret good turn.

"Best duster," she said, nodding sheepishly. "I was gonna dust your high places where you can't get ..."

A hatch! Nora's face was at a hatch which handed through into the living room, something Janey had missed completely. Stupid! How could that happen and her reckon herself to be good at this?

Who had rotten hatches except on the telly? But she was proud of the best dusters touch. Her nan had always kept one for bits of china, treated it like the scarves and hankies.

"Do them another day, eh? I'll have to rinse one through. But mind your water, Kelly, dear ..."

Janey looked at the bucket in the sink. It was full and the water was splashing everywhere. "Ooer!" She laughed, a sort of snort. "My nan used to say I was strong in the heart but weak in the head!" She rushed over and turned off the tap.

"I'm sure that's not true, lovie."

Janey threw herself into her mopping. "Won't be long. You can come back in a minute."

"Let it have a good dry. I don't want to go base over apex. Plenty of time, lovie."

The old woman disappeared and Janey worked on, humming, disappointed that this time the old girl had left the hatch wide open.

Still, it hadn't been a complete waste of her time, Janey decided. Look on the bright side: she'd ruled out the favourite place: unless the money was in the other drawer, she was just going to have to look somewhere else; like upstairs, by the old girl's bed. So at least she knew what she had to do next. She picked up a spoon from the draining board. "Now, where do you go, spoon?" she asked in a good, loud voice. "In here?" She opened the second drawer. Hankies, scarves and folded paper bags. No, not in here. And the spoon went where commonsense said, in the cutlery drawer at the sink.

So she'd better try upstairs now, if she was going to get what she wanted today. But how to get up there? That was the problem. Unless she offered to mop over the bathroom floor.

By the time the kitchen was dry and put back to rights, though, and they were smiling at each other over glasses of milk, Janey had got it worked out, had decided on a better way of getting herself into the bedrooms.

"That window," she said, twinkling her eyes, "up your stairs. I think that's really nice . . ."

She couldn't have said a better thing. It was as if she'd touched a button connected up to the old woman's heart. "Oh, do you like it? I might have known you'd be the sort who would." Nora Woodcroft's face seemed to shed ten years as she leant forward and covered Janey's hand with her own, like someone passing some sort of secret good news. "Do you know, that window is why we moved here in the first place, Alfred and me. We were out for a walk and we saw it, first thing after the 'For Sale' sign, and did we argue about it, what the picture meant!" She giggled as she recalled their early married delight in things. "He said one thing and I said another. Till we plucked up courage and knocked to enquire about the house for sale, just to find out. And although moving house was the last thing on earth we meant to do, we ended up buying it and brought up a daughter here . . ."

"I dunno what it means. Can I go up and have a look at it? Up close?"

"Of course you can, poppet. What a pleasure for someone to ask. There's so much taken for granted these days. You shall have a close look with the light shining in behind it. And I'll come and tell you all about it."

Janey's protest sounded a bit too loud. "No, you save your legs. I'll have a good look, then you tell me when I get back down."

"How considerate! But I'll not be an invalid for anyone. Come on," she said to herself, "put your best foot forward, girl."

Janey, laughed, high and false, had to pretend to be pleased: but with the old lady's legs being bad, she'd banked everything on going up on her own. As it was, she'd have done better to offer to mop the bathroom.

What happened was an eye-opener, all the same. After the hatch, Janey shouldn't have been surprised at anything about Nora Woodcroft and this house: but she hadn't bargained for the shock of seeing her get up to that landing. Her mouth dropped wide open as she watched. Whatever was up with the old lady on the level it definitely didn't work the same on the stairs. After a slow walk along the hall, just the same as before, with Janey following like a nurse with a patient, at the bottom of the stairs Nora suddenly let go of her walker, grabbed at the banister, and fairly scampered up to the landing, pulling hard with her arms and pushing with her feet as sure as Janey in the gym.

"See? It's not really my feet that's up with me. It's here – in here!" Nora tapped her forehead. "This is what needs sorting out."

The girl could only stare. The old woman wasn't even out of breath: and it was a good job Janey had seen it or she could have been well caught out upstairs: thought she was safe and got surprised by how quick Nora was.

"Yeah, you done that all right."

But with the shock over, there was no way Janey's attention could stay off that huge window a moment longer. It made a cathedral of the landing. With the October sun low in the sky and misty, it sent a strong, well-spread light filtering through the picture, cast patches of blue and red and green onto the carpet, the walls, the stairs, it painted colours on arms and faces, and spread a strange sense of peace and calm over the two of them, and over the house.

"Oh, that's really lovely."

Nora Woodcroft sat on a stair and motioned for Janey to sit down beside her.

"Now, Kelly, how well do you know your Bible?"

"Oh, not all that special," Janey said, pulling a face. "Christmas and Easter and things like that, and Moses . . . and Adam and Eve. Just the usual, you know . . ."

"How about the story of Ruth?"

Janey shook her head. "Don't think so. Heard of her, like."

"Well, this – " Nora Woodcroft waved at the picture in front of her, which even as she spoke was changing its colours with the sinking of the sun – "this is the story of Ruth." She paused while Janey took it in. "There," she said, pointing to a central, stooped character, "that's Ruth, gleaning in the fields . . ."

"Yeah?"

"Following the line of harvesters." The old lady was miles away now; while from the corner of her eye, to her left, Janey could see quite clearly a wide open door and a big bed in the room beyond. *Her* bedroom, and really close, it looked: just where Janey wanted to get her nose in, and only feet away . . .

"It's a lovely story. You know what she did? Ruth? She stuck by her mother-in-law through thick and thin, wouldn't abandon her, no matter what." Nora closed her eyes. " 'Where you go, I will go, and where you stay, I will stay. Your people shall be my people, and your God my God. Where you die, I will die . . !' " There was a sudden catch in her voice, and she stopped; took a few seconds to compose herself. "Stupid old thing I am, I can never say that without filling up . . . but they *are* lovely words, aren't they, Kelly?"

She took Janey's hand and squeezed it; held it in her lap while she rocked to and fro like getting a baby off to sleep and stared at the picture which was fading away into night.

"See, and there she is, breaking her back, picking up bits and pieces of barley the reapers have missed, to take home and share with her mother-in-law . . ."

"Yeah . . ."

She squeezed Janey's hand tighter, hurt her with the intensity of it.

"She must'a been good . . ."

62

"She was. And she got her reward, too, in the end. But I won't bore you with it now." She suddenly snapped back to the present. "I'm going down to put the kettle on. Do you know I've upset myself? Just because you wanted to see the window. Silly old woman, aren't I?"

"No. No, you ain't . . . "

Nora let go of Janey's hand and pulled herself up. "But you stay here. Just watch the way the last thing to catch the light is that moon." She pointed to a disc in the stained-glass sky, about half as big as a saucer. "It's supposed to be the sun, really, in the daytime. But when the real sun goes down that little circle's the last thing to take the light, being high up: and it seems to work by magic to turn the whole picture into night. You watch. My own Ruth used to sit here with her mouth open, watching that . . . "

Quietly, sniffing a bit, Nora took herself to the foot of the stairs: while with one eye still on the moon, Janey watched her go, saw her suddenly turn to a cripple again as she got to the flat and had to start manoeuvring her walking frame.

"A bit of loyalty," Nora called up. "I'd swap a kingdom for it." And with a metallic step, slide, step, slide, she made her laboured way back to the kitchen.

The old woman wasn't out of sight a second before Janey jumped up from the window and crept to the bedroom door. There was still enough light to see the big bed neatly made, and to see the things on the bedside table. A clock, a glass – and a fat leather handbag. And now Janey knew. There were no two ways about it: that was where the business was; her pension book and her envelopes of cash. And going by that big reward there ought to be enough in there to keep Reggie quiet *and* give her a start at the club with Mary. What was more she could be out of the house and away with it hours before the old girl came to bed and even guessed at what she'd done. And it'd all be dead easy, too, because she'd hear her coming a mile off with the warning that frame would give along the wooden hall floor. No nasty surprises with a hatch up here, not as long as she kept her ears open.

Janey stood in the bedroom doorway and took a last look back towards the big picture window. She listened hard, heard the clunk of a kettle on a tap, waited for the water running. A slight lean of her body and she could see down the stairs, double-check that the coast was still clear.

Right! Go! Eh? Go! she told herself. Back into the bedroom, over to that big bag and do the business. O.K! Go then! Now was the golden opportunity to rush in and rush out with the loot, what she'd come for, quick and easy. She willed it, she wanted it. But for some reason, in a weird way, her feet just would not move. Go! blast you, go! She swore at them, tried to kick them off, pushed her body forward to get them moving across the flat carpet of the bedroom. But they wouldn't take her, it was as if they were rooted there, just like the old woman's when she was standing on her own without her frame. Janey was stuck, her feet could have been buried to the ankles in soft sand. And it wasn't any magic, she knew; nothing stupid like that. It was something inside her head telling her no. There was no way she was going to make it through that bedroom door.

The other way, though, that was different. Back down a step of the landing to the window was another matter altogether. Besides which, there was no alternative. So she found herself going that way, angry, frustrated; left the bedroom and thumped herself down, and with all sorts of turmoil going on inside, she did what the old lady had told her; stared at the weird effect as the last of the light turned the sun into the moon somehow to make the picture all different, with Ruth breaking her back in the night, still picking up barley for the old woman. When all at once her disappointment went and a new calm feeling seemed to wash over her. Reggie – and Mary – could have been a million miles away, and for five peaceful minutes she didn't want for anything in the world.

FIVE

She thought Reggie was going to murder her. When she tried to tell him she'd had no luck, his eyes seemed to shrivel like currants and the pupils went to sharp pinpoints of pure hate. He'd been waiting for her, dressed in his best leather to go and throw the money at Kipper. But she came home with nothing, with not so much as ten pence, and she thought herself lucky to get away in one piece.

Janey hadn't grown up in that house, though, doing the things they all did, without learning a thing or two about surviving. Walking home she'd worked it out that the last thing Reggie was going to want was Lou knowing about any of this. Because if he did, Lou, who'd fixed his eye on the house in the first place, who'd watched it on and off for a couple of weeks, would definitely want to be in on any money coming out of it. She could almost hear him saying: "What d'you reckon I done all that for, my rotten 'ealth?" So she knew what her best tactics were. Make a lot of noise going in, call out to Lou to find out where he was, and make sure she was never too far away from where he could hear her.

As it happened, he was in the kitchen, making himself a sandwich. She could smell Marmite being spread the minute she came in through the front door: and she knew how much Reggie loathed the stuff. She'd just got into the passage when the skinhead came racing down the stairs as if he'd done a murder in the bedroom, his leather creaking and his face all tense. "Well? You got it?" he hissed.

Janey shook her head, slipped out from under the hand which grabbed at her shoulder, and got as near as she could to the kitchen door.

"Went right through the kitchen," she hissed at him. "Couldn't get no farther. Turned it inside out, but not a sniff down there. I'm goin' back Wednesday, though."

65

"Wednesday?" Reggie croaked. "What good's poxy Wednesday? Derry or someone'll 'ave that bike by then!" Glaring his murderous look he suddenly grabbed her by the shoulder. "You get back there now. Make up some story: get looking round upstairs, you 'ear me?" He pushed and pulled her shoulder, digging in his nails, hurting.

"Ow! You! Reggie!" she shouted.

It did what she wanted. Through a mouthful of bread and Marmite Lou started shouting, too. "Janey, stop bloody messin' about an' come 'ere!"

For a second Janey could see Reggie weighing up whether to give her a final clout. But he must have thought he might still have something to lose because he contented himself with mouthing an obscene name in her face and then he let her go. In an instant Janey had slipped in through the kitchen door and was leaning looking at Lou. "Yeah?" she asked, against the smack and swallow of his chewing. She looked into his blue eyes, saw his face shaved shiny smooth, the thick head of close-cut black hair: a fair-looking bloke when her mum had met him. He burped on his bread.

"Been waitin' for you. Where you been?"

Janey gave him the answer she'd had ready, straight off the top like a trick card. "Homework," she said, "round Mary's. Do 'ave to do some, you know."

"Yeah, well, too much brainwork ain't good for you. Brings you out in spots." The big man got up. "Come on, I got an 'ouse to try: big one, over Plumstead. Grab yourself a bite 'an we'll get off."

Janey did as she was told. She didn't give it a second thought, any more than she ever had. Why should she? It'd keep her out of Reggie's way. Besides, this was how they earned their living, wasn't it? She'd have no trouble knocking over a stranger's house. It was only that old lady's bedroom her feet had refused to take her into.

66

Ruth and John Seymore sat in canvas chairs at the side of the tennis arena and watched Samantha hit from the baseline: her dress and her stance pure Wimbledon: her play a lot nearer the public courts.

"That was out!" she screeched at the umpire. "Hell, can't you see that line?"

But while John quietly groaned, Ruth heard none of it. She was there in body because good parents came to Tournament Nights: but she had no more idea of the score than the stewards serving the drinks.

"John, I know it's a disappointment. I know how you deserve the break. But honestly, I'm her only one. And she is my mother . . ."

John's programme was screwed in his hand. "I know, I know." He was torn between the two dramas being played: his daughter's on the court and his wife's by his side. "*Sammy, that was a let, now play it and don't argue, honey.* It's just that the letter from the church and the letters from her don't seem to describe the same person. She sounds just fine when she writes to you. She sounded fine when you phoned her; firm, strong voice and all, you said so. What I'm trying to say is, she could come over for a good, long stay when we get back from the West Coast and we can judge how she is for ourselves."

"John, I *know*. It's a daughter's instinct. I *know* she's covering up. I've told her about our vacation and she just doesn't want to spoil it. You know what she's like. But what would people say if anything happened to her while we're off having a good time?"

"That was a good service!" Samantha shouted. "How can you say that was *out*?"

"All right," John gave in, "you go, then. I told you when we came over, any time you're worried . . . go sort things out." His tone softened and he reached for her hand. "Hell, I know she's your mother. I know you've got to do what's best, I know that. O.K., look round a few places, find out what the nursing homes cost, talk to her about coming here. Find out all you can, cover all the angles, then we can discuss it. Now, how's that?"

67

Ruth Seymore sat back in her chair. "Thank you, John. You've put my mind at rest. I can relax if I know what I'm doing is best." She blinked, re-focused her eyes in a big show of looking. "Now, tell me quick, who's winning this match?"

John watched a long lob go into the upper tier.

"Let's say we won't need to stop her off for Nevr-Dull on the way home. There's not going to be any trophies to polish tonight . . ."

Ruth sighed. "Oh dear," she said, "and I turned her out looking like a real champion. Just make sure we get a photograph, will you. Something to take for Mother to see. You know how proud she always likes to feel . . ."

It was a close thing as to who looked forward to Wednesday more: Janey, with a certain freedom from knowing her feet wouldn't let her rob the old woman whatever Reggie threatened, and Nora, with a delight in the young company which put her so much in mind of her own childhood.

At Janey's school the maths teacher was away that morning, but Janey worked out a few sums of her own and she was quite pleased with the result. Three times a week at the old woman's was quite a stint, it struck her, and it could definitely be on the cards that over the course of a fortnight or so she could earn what she needed for the Deptford Centre. If she got two pounds a night that'd make six for the week, so if someone halfway nice gave her time enough to pay she could soon sort out sufficient to keep on level pegging with Mary. Perhaps her stupid feet had been right all the time and she could actually afford to *like* going to the old woman's: perhaps Reggie would forget after a couple of days and she could relax and enjoy the chocolate biscuits, the lemonade and the talks. God knew, she'd had nothing like it since Nan Pearce had gone.

Paper darts and swear words flew about among the books while Janey's maths set wasted half-an-hour in the library.

But with Mary in a higher set she was ignored and left to sit in peace and think about Nora and her nan.

Nan Pearce had been a great old girl; her real dad's mother who'd never got over the shock of him upping and going to Australia. "Wasn't even deported!" Nan Pearce had told her cronies. "But then with a wife like that, can you blame the boy?" It was about that time, perhaps because of him, that Lou had walked in with Reggie, but Nan Pearce had died of a stroke and neglect before she'd had to tell Janey not to let him near her: and thank God, hers was one house Reggie had never got into to foul up.

But over all the years, Nan Pearce had had a lot of time for her boy's Janey. She'd always be getting things out for her, showing her old treasures, telling her things, whispering secrets, treating her the way grandchildren either hate or they love; and which Janey had loved. She'd even talked about leaving her something when she went, but the end had come very suddenly; and the grabbing aunts and uncles had crawled out of the woodwork, and with Janey's mum gone too, hadn't even told Janey the day of the funeral. The last time Janey had cried had been to mourn her old nan on the quiet, in bed, without letting Reggie hear.

So when Nora, just the same in lots of ways, had wanted her back, had done things like showing her the little statue, had sat and explained the picture window the same way her nan would have done, suddenly it had all seemed too good for anyone to spoil: not Lou, not Reggie, and especially not Janey herself. And now going back had turned into a treat. All the time she could push Reggie to the back of her mind, she could sit and wait for the four o'clock buzzer with the same impatience as everyone else.

It was a chillier day, one of those when Nora thought to look out her heavier coat, wondered about re-making her bed with the electric blanket in it. She looked at her sprinkling of soot and tossed up whether to give the chimney a surprise with a real fire. Well, wouldn't that be nice for young Kelly? she thought: the girl could fill up with coal, wash over the hearth, polish the fender; and then they could sit and toast bread for their tea: just like the old days before all this central heating: just like she'd done as a girl for a Saturday treat.

But her face fell when she realised there wasn't any wood – she seemed to put off thinking about winter till later each year – so they'd just have to be content round the electric. What a shame, though ...

She was in the front room waiting when Janey rang the bell that day, watching through the nets like an outpatient for the ambulance. Janey hardly had time to lean on the porch before the door suddenly swung open.

"Christ, that was quick!" the girl said. "Er, my goodness!"

Nora smiled. Everyone slipped, didn't they, especially poor little devils who knew no better? "Come in, lovie; I was waiting for you, watching out the window like some Nosey Parker!"

"I come as quick as I could. Only, some ol' dear kept us back to give out Open Day letters."

"Oh, and when's that? I hope you get a good report."

"Not sure. I lost mine." It had gone in a ball down a drain. "So what you want doin' today?" She smiled as she said it, made a helpful face for the old woman.

Put on the spot so quickly, Nora stood in her frame like someone in the dock. "I don't know," she said, flustered, "I'll have to think. I'll tell you what was in my mind, till the penny dropped I'd got no wood ... " She told Janey her original plan, with a promise that they'd do it the next time she came, after the coalman had brought her some wood.

But Janey was smiling, shaking her head. "We can do it now if you like," she said, "you don't need no wood. I know a good way. My nan never bought no firewood. Wouldn't waste money on it. You got any old papers?"

Nora suddenly left her frame to itself to clap her hands in delight. "I know!" she said. "Don't tell me!" She pointed at Janey. "Crackers!" And she laughed. "Not you, lovie, that's what we used to call them. And I'd forgotten! All those years . . . That's a trick my old dad taught me."

"Yeah, crackers."

Janey led the way to the kitchen. "You do forget," she said over her shoulder, " 'less you got some reason to remember. Now, let's see if you do 'em the same way as me . . . "

With several old newspapers which Nora dug out of a cupboard, Janey began making the fire-lighting crackers the way her nan had once shown her. She folded the spread paper diagonally in inch-and-a-half strips getting thicker and thicker, thumbed the long shape flat and finally wound it round and round her hand to make a tight circlet of newsprint.

"There y'are!" she said. "*News of the World's* best, my nan used to reckon. " 'Rude stuff always burns slow,' she said." Janey looked at the newspaper she'd worked on. "But I 'spect the *Mail's* just as good . . . "

"Not a lot to choose between any of them these days." Nora looked at the finished product held flat on a proud palm. "But that's it, lovie, that's just how I remember doing them. Except we tucked our ends in." She took the cracker and tucked the outside ends into the centre, finally compressing the whole thing to make a neat, tight shape. "There!" She winked at Janey. "Who says some of the old tricks don't come in handy? Now what say we go the whole hog and make a grate-full?"

Without speaking, the two of them grabbed a sheet of paper each and began making their fire-lighters, blacking their fingers with printers' ink, smearing their faces where they touched, using sheet after sheet of paper until three old *Mails* were used up and lying like a nest of paper serpents coiled in the wood basket in the front room.

"How's that for a good job done?" Nora sat back with her hands in her lap: and without bothering to have the fender polished or the hearth washed over, she sent Janey for some coal and accepted help being lowered to the hearth rug; where, like a couple of excited children, they built the fire and set light to it, anxious to see if the old trick still worked.

They watched every movement as the smoke twisted up slowly in its search for the little-used chimney, as the coiled paper stiffened and browned and blackened into small flames and the fire ate into its tight layers. Coal settled, tumbled, fell out into the hearth, and it was a race between them to get the first hand to it to throw it back: no tongs but licked fingers till the heat got hold: sitting side by side on the hearth rug like a scene from a Victorian story book.

"It's going a treat!" said Nora. "Fancy you remembering crackers – oh, you are a clever girl."

Janey smiled modestly: she was pleased it had gone well; not like at her nan's sometimes when they'd had to fall back on drawing up the fire dangerously with big sheets of paper.

The coal took, dusty sparks began to fly and some settled to glow in the soot at the back of the fireplace. "Look!" Janey pointed. "Fairies!" Before she remembered how old she was and went red.

Nora exclaimed, swayed on the floor from her picnic position and would have clapped her hands if she'd had one to spare. "You're right! Fairies! I haven't thought about fire-fairies in years!" She swayed into Janey, steadied herself with a hand round the girl's shoulder and found herself hugging her hard. "Wish!" she said. "You have to wish when you see one of those."

Janey closed her eyes but didn't know what to wish for. It was hard to put into the words of a wish all the things she wanted. So she pretended; opened her eyes after a few seconds and said, "Done it!"

"And I pray it comes true," said Nora, still holding her. And in a sudden impulse she kissed Janey on her coal-smeared cheek and squeezed her till she shook. "Because I do believe mine has already ... "

While Janey, who hadn't been kissed in over two years, could only stare into the flames for fear of crying.

"Don't half go, your fire," she said at last. "Throws out a good heat, an' all." At which they both remembered they'd been going to make toast, and Janey gave Nora the hand up she couldn't do without.

If the Woolwich skins thought they were street-wise, Reggie had a street brain that put him in the *Mastermind* class. People had to get up early to put one over on him. He could read situations from round the corner: he was only ever caught off balance when it was some part of his plan: he knew when the opposition was weak enough for him to stay and fight and he knew when it was strong enough to cut out and run. He knew what weapon to carry and he knew where to carry it. Most important of all, he knew what people's weaknesses were. And that was what made him so dangerous.

He knew that Spiros Kiperanous's strength was his family: his big Greek father and his brothers who, like some easy-going Mafia, always seemed to protect him. But Kipper's weakness was a Turkish girl called Selda, and from what the kids said his father would have killed him for it: or, at least, cut him out of the business. Meanwhile, everyone knew Kipper was daft over the girl, and now Reggie was going to play on it.

He caught Kipper coming out of the park, a mile from his father's take-away, all very public and open, about to mount the Kawasaki and go and do his stuff on the doners. But because he'd spied, because he'd seen, Reggie knew who was leaving the park by the other gate.

"Gettin' a bit cold for all that i'n it, Kip? Touch o' frost where you don' want it?"

Spiros smiled, caught off guard, eyes all round for who was with Reggie. "Leave off! What do you want round here anyway?"

"I wanna talk about this, don' I?" Reggie stood with his hands on the handlebars, legs straddling the front wheel. "An' her." He jerked his head in the direction of the park.

"I don't get you. I don't get what you're getting at, Reggie." But Kipper did. It was in his eyes.

"It's easy, Kip. I wanna buy your bike. No favours, the full asking price, what you was asking last week. That's what I want. An' what you *don't* want is your old man knowing about your little bit o' Turkish Delight over there. Right? Now I'd 'a thought that was dead easy to get . . ."

Spiros stared at Reggie. "Be fair, I want a quick sale, son, an' you ain't bein' quick. Bloke's pushing me for the money, else I lose my new one." There was a full kneel of pleading in his voice.

Reggie wrinkled his nose. "Then stall him, eh, Kipper? Hang 'im on for a bit. Else, I don't know, but you might lose plenty more'n your new bike, eh?"

The two of them stared each other out: until Reggie ended it by slowly unstraddling his leg and releasing his grip on the handlebars.

Angrily, Spiros kick-started the machine.

"Starts a real treat," Reggie said. "Even in the cold. I reckon I'm gettin' a fair bargain there."

After the pleasure of Wednesday, the next morning Nora felt all anyhow. At best it was one of those middle-of-the-week days which she was pleased just to get through: so many hours of routine before she went back to bed again: but today seemed even emptier without Kelly coming. She'd got up, forced herself to change her sheets and put her electric blanket in, chewed at a bit of breakfast, looked out at the same view of long grass in the garden, thrown bread out to attract some birds and aimlessly gone from room to room to see what there was to do without feeling the least little bit like doing it.

She'd stayed in the front room; sat there in the cold and looked at the day-after grate. She'd thought about Miss Stephenson's visit, the old interferer, and thought how even a *friendly* call from the Ladies' League would have been nice. They didn't have to attack the place like Task Force: just coming to talk would have done.

And her mind had gone back to Kelly, the girl from the council houses who might show them all how she could manage.

She was a fly little thing. Nothing much got missed by those sharp young eyes, and that was a fact. They were here, there and everywhere, taking it all in, not missing a trick. And interested in people, had a bit of time for her. That made a change these days, a kiddie who didn't write you off because you were old. Poor little tyke. Not much of a home life, Nora thought, apart from the grandmother. Mother none too special, you could tell that; and no doubt one of a dozen or so brothers and sisters; they always were. Nora swayed her head to a rhythm without a tune. Wouldn't she take to a proper upbringing, a girl like that. A bit of real looking after . . . Nora sighed. Well, it'd be tomorrow before Kelly came again. Mondays, Wednesdays and Fridays and a five pound note in her hand for the weekend. Not a fortune for all the pleasure *she'd* get from it, but probably be like gold-dust to the girl . . . Which reminded her. She'd better have some money handy: just a bit to see her over the week-end, something to send Kelly shopping with and a bit for odd bills.

Nora pulled herself up and balanced herself back in her frame. Even this took more out of her today, she thought, as she stood and shook and summoned the will to make her legs move and jerk the thing forward. There were no two ways about it. On a bad day everything was harder.

But she didn't get the money: didn't go to the secret place where she kept it: because when she got into the passage the second post had been delivered, and lying there on the mat was one of the things she lived for: a familiar piece of crinkly paper: an air mail letter from Canada.

The frame seemed to do a jig of its own down the hall and Nora didn't notice how quickly her feet took her back to the kitchen. "Oh, thank you, thank you," she said to the ceiling – waving the thin paper like a coronation flag. "You *do* answer prayers." But if she was pleased at seeing the envelope with that familiar handwriting on it, she was upset and angry when she tore it open and saw what Ruth's letter said inside.

Dear Mother, (that always sounded strange from the start: why couldn't she still say 'Mum'?) *This is sooner than my usual letter and is written to say what I should have said on the transatlantic phone. But I thought you sounded shaky and I didn't want to upset you . . .*

Shaky? Nora Woodcroft frowned. It was only her legs that played her up. Her hands and her voice were all right, thank you very much. *Pleased* is what she'd been, not shaky!

I've had a letter from the church, from Miss Stephenson, a very nice-sounding woman, and sensible. She's taken the trouble to write to say that you're a bit unsteady these days, not quite your old self. Don't get her wrong, or me, she's just concerned that you might have a fall all alone in that house and there wouldn't be anyone near enough to hear you.

With a rude word she rarely used, Nora flapped the letter on the table, stared at the sheet and pulled an ugly, angry face at it. "Busybody, busybody, busybody!" She banged her fist on the table. "BUSYBODY!"

So don't take it amiss, but Sammy and I are flying over really soon to see you. Just a little break to show Sammy more of London, catch up with the museums, and have a look at how you are. She went on to give details of flights and times. And the rest was routine news. Samantha being pipped at the singles tournament but not having a partner for the doubles. John working hard. How the P.T.A. were appointing a new principal at Samantha's school. But Nora wasn't fooled. She knew all of that was just to fill the standard air mail form, to make it all look normal. The bombshell had been at the beginning.

She sat there in the kitchen and stared into space, didn't know whether to laugh or to cry. It was wonderful news that she'd see Ruth again, and Samantha all grown-up by three years: usually she'd ring round anyone she knew, distant cousins she didn't see from one year's end to the next, just to share the news. But this visit was different. Very different. This visit was an *inspection*. What a blessed nerve! Nora got angrier the more she thought about it. There she was, a full-grown

woman, completely sound of mind and all but a little sound of
body, about to be looked at with a view to . . . what? The writing
a blur, she turned her head and focused on her frame. With a
view to seeing whether she should be allowed to carry on living
the way she did or be stuck in an old people's home somewhere!
That's what it amounted to. An inspection to decide whether
she kept or lost her independence, whether or not she should go
on being in control over her own life!

For a while she sat there with her mouth set, her eyes angry,
straight and independent in the middle of her own kitchen,
where she'd bathed children and cooked Christmas dinners for
twelve. And then she cried. She cried like anyone does who's
about to lose their most precious possession. Because in this
letter she could see that everyone else thought she'd come to the
end of her road, and other people were going to decide her
future. She looked around at what she'd built up and realised
what an awful thought that was. Like losing citizenship, or
being certified insane. She could see herself being carried
screaming out of this place.

Within an hour, though, she had begun to recover. Perhaps it
had been good that the tears had all come out. Who knew?
Perhaps with self-pity out of the way, it had been easier to dry
her eyes, take a nip or two of brandy, screw up the letter – the
only letter from Ruth she hadn't treasured – and decide that
Nora Woodcroft was ready. Ready for a fight!

She got up, steadied herself and looked at the calendar
Sammy had made. The thirteenth. When was that? Monday
week. Good Lord, that was quick! Ruth wasn't letting the grass
grow under her feet, was she? But all right. It still gave her time,
just about. She'd sort things out by that Monday or she'd die in
the attempt. She gripped her frame like a chariot and made a
Boadicea face. Because when she did die she was going to die
here, where she'd lived: not in some old people's home and
certainly not half a world away in Canada. Lonely or not, this
was the place, because this was the place that was home. Just a
bit of help, that's all she needed, and she'd got that in willing

77

little Kelly. So let the rest watch out, the whole lot of them! And alone or not, defiant, she suddenly wanted to cheer.

Old Mary looked all right in her school uniform, Janey reckoned. That sort of thing suited her, it pulled her into shape, flattened her a bit like her leotard did, made her more of a piece. Her own would have hung off her, if she'd had one, would never have looked right; but Mary could definitely wear a uniform. And from the sounds of it, wearing a blazer and skirt had been a good idea, turning up for the test looking smart, marching in like they do when they parade round the stadium for the Games. She only needed a flag to carry, Mary said. Made her really feel the part.

"But how d'you get on when you actually done your test?"

"Dunno, they didn't say. You give 'em money for the stamp an' they write to you."

"Yeah, but *you* know, don't you? If you'd 'a kept losing your balance you'd know. What you have to do?"

"Bit of floor stuff, cartwheel, handstand, forward roll an' a handstand bridge to stand up. That was all right. Then a squat vault an' a straddle, and just a bit on the beam – mount turn and jump, and a cartwheel dismount if you wanted."

"That ain't bad. I dunno about the cartwheel dismount. Did they look strict?"

"Yeah, there was four of them. I dunno who was, like, the one, but they all looked proper, kept marking things – talking and never endin' pointing. All the mums was getting real jittery ..."

"Did your mum go?"

"Yeah. Course. What sort of a mum...?" Mary's hand shot to her mouth: her face said she knew she'd tripped on the mat. "But she'll go with you, an' all, she told me ..."

Janey couldn't help laughing. "They'll know she ain't my mum, 'less they're colour blind!"

Mary laughed. "Anyhow, we put your name down. So when you gonna go for it, Janey?"

"I'll wait and see how you get on."

"No, you don't wanna leave it, Janey, 'cos they'll fill up with rubbish if you ain't quick. You promise. Don't leave it long, girl, eh?"

They were sitting there in the quiet, now, with Mary's mother gone to her Baptist meeting and Mr Richards off at work: but tapes and dancing and being free to go in the front room were all forgotten tonight, because both of them knew that Mary would do it: whatever Janey decided, Mary would definitely join the gymnastics thing.

Tonight, though, down inside Janey had hope. "I'm not gonna leave it long. It's what I come to tell you. I think I can raise the money. I'm picking up extra for a few nights down at my old lady's; that's why I can't hang about too long, as it goes ..."

"Yeah?" Mary relaxed: she found some sweets in a dish. "What you do down there? Tell us."

"Well, all sorts. She's got this big house, and this big garden. And she reckons they all think it's too much, like, and someone's comin' to put her in a home – or they *might* like – 'less she shows 'em how good she can get on, on her own."

"Yeah? They done that to my auntie ... "

"So, anyhow, I've got to help her do her garden, run some old lawnmower over it, or something." Janey snorted. "Anyhow, she's gonna pay me extra, the weekend. So, bit of luck, never know, I'll be down Deptford doing that test next week ... "

"Yeah?" Mary jumped up. "Janey, be great, eh? What night, Wednesday or Thursday?"

"Dunno. Soon as I can, anyhow. Just keep your fingers crossed she gives me plenty. Would you reckon it, though, Janey Pearce doing gardening? Dunno about joining gymnastics, I'll be watchin' *Blue Peter* 'fore you know it!"

Mary laughed; and Janey felt good. Because that was how

79

she liked it: her and Mary laughing together and nothing coming in between.

Janey had never had much time for a close-up look at long grass: she hadn't led that sort of life. In her paintings, when she had to do art, the sky was blue and the grass was green, and keep your fingers crossed one didn't run into the other. Where Janey grew up earth was dirt and flowers were for funerals. But on the Monday she found out all about long grass at first hand. Leaving the school after her dinner, she'd run straight round to the old lady's, told her a lie about a staff meeting giving them all the afternoon off, and offered to get on with the gardening. "Give us a bit more time, eh? Break the back of it, like, 'cos there's tons to do 'fore next week ..."

Janey had caught Nora in one of her despairing moods, after a restless week-end when everything needing to be done had gone round and round inside her head. She'd lain in bed, staring at the ceiling and worried herself sick about the future. Let Ruth look *anywhere*, she'd thought, and she could find her wanting. She could drive a coach and horses through things: through big things, like the damp down the bedroom wall; through small things, like losing the run of her television licence; through silly things, like not having a proper top to her jam dish. So when she'd seen Kelly turning up out of the blue she'd clapped her hands and shouted, "My angel's come!"

It was a beautiful afternoon, one of October's best, a warm sun and no wind. And even in the front garden with its high overgrown hedges they were as secluded as in some quiet country village. Janey could actually hear birds above the noise of the buses. Nora showed her where the lawnmower was and carefully lowered herself to the grass by an old seat. "Don't you do a dash without helping me up," she said, "or I'm stuck down here till Doomsday!" And she'd suddenly laughed like a conspirator and started snapping at the edges with a pair of rusty shears.

80

Janey had never realised that grass had so many different sorts of tops, that it could be thin and tough, wide and flat, deep green and yellow-white, could cut your finger, even. She only ever went on mowed stuff at the school field: she'd never realised that these long stalks like harvest came from the same sort of plant. But she had guessed about the lawnmower. The clattering old machine either clogged itself up or skidded across the bent wet stalks: there was no pushing it, no getting anywhere with it, not the first time over. So Janey took over the shears and Nora crawled along on all fours pulling up clumps out of old flower beds with her bare hands. It was hard, back-breaking work, trying to surprise the grass into getting itself clipped, and more often than not Janey missed biting at it altogether. Her picture of a neat, trim lawn and extra cash in her hand quickly faded, and she knew it would be Wednesday at the earliest before the old girl said, "Well done, Kelly." It was all getting a bit heavy when suddenly, in the middle of a sore-handed struggle where the shears were giving best to a thick clump of grass, Janey heard the choke: a throaty sort of gurgle, and a moan with a scream in it. In a fright, she let the grass go and turned round – to see the old lady rolling over on her back, still clutching a bunch of weeds in her hand, flattening the grass with her body. Janey dropped the shears and rushed over. "Here, you all right?" She forced herself to look at the reddened old face, squinting her eyes in defence against what she might see. And she stared down at Nora Woodcroft shaking, helpless with laughter.

"Have you ever seen ... such a *pantomime*?" she croaked. "I ask you! Could we ... could we have made it look blessed worse if we'd tried?" Janey frowned at the old woman, who was clutching her stomach with the pain of the laughter. "Bless you for trying, but look! Two good hearts ... a rusty pair of shears ... a clapped-out lawnmower ... and the biggest shambles in south London!" She cackled again, making loud satisfying 'aaah' sounds on each indrawn breath.

Janey gave an eye to the garden. The old girl was dead right. It was a right old mess! They'd had a go here and had a go there, but it was all bits and pieces, piles of pulled-up clumps and half-chewed handfuls lying about in a trampled patch of grass with earth and stones scattered all over it. Janey put a hand on a hip and leant her weight on one leg. "Yeah," she said. "See what you mean!"

"No offence, love, but it's like one of those modern hair-styles. One bit doesn't know what the next bit's doing. Oh my God, help me up. They're probably right. I must be going round the bend."

Still laughing in spasms, Nora got to the path and sat there, legs wide like a baby, and waited patiently while Janey helped get her up with the kitchen chair she'd brought out.

"Don't get me wrong, you've worked hard, Kelly, and I feel mean for laughing." She took in a big breath. "But if you don't see the funny side you might as well curl up and die, don't you think?"

"Yeah. It needs a sickle, or a hovercraft thing. Wouldn't be so bad then."

Nora chuckled again. "Atom bomb more like!" But suddenly her mood changed. She stopped and her face became serious. "Oh, if my Alfred could see me now! All this palaver – to stay here in our own house." She waved at the old building in front of them.

Janey's thin spine stood straight, she felt the warmth of the sun through her dress as she turned to where that big stained-glass window took her eye again.

"I tell you what," she said, "what all that grass cutting says to you: picking up them bits o' corn all day long, bending down, 'ow that old Ruth must've sweated. Bloomin' hard work, i'n it?"

The sun sent a sparkle off Nora's frame as she turned it to stand and squint at Janey. "What an intelligent thing to say. You're right, Kelly. You understand things . . ."

Janey let a shoulder drop: said nothing: didn't feel like it for a moment.

"Yeah!" A loud voice broke the silence. It came from the gap in the hedge where the gate was. And suddenly in strutted Reggie – boots, khaki trousers, singlet with a Union Jack displayed. "Yeah, sussed this had to be the place."

Nora's squint in the sun was a frown now, and she was standing up very straight behind her chair, gripping the seat with a hand.

"'S'all right, don' stand on ceremony. Knew this was it, didn't I?" He stood there, nodding and chewing. "Nice big place you got, missus . . ."

Janey was lost for words: couldn't think of a single thing to say. The stupid idiot coming here! She'd been stalling him all week, telling him a load of lies and thinking he'd gone off the idea. But he hadn't, by the looks of it. Now what if he went and used her name? He could blow the lot, the great berk!

"Doin' a bit o' gardening?" Reggie sniggered. "Ain't got far, 'ave you? You need a proper thing for that grass."

"That's just what we were saying, wasn't it, Kelly?"

Reggie looked at Janey and sniggered again. He'd got the message. He wasn't thick, that was his trouble.

"Well, yeah. Only I was goin' by, an' looked through the gate, an' you didn't look like you was getting very far. 'Cos you know I could do you a day, Saturday if you like. Put a bit o' beef in that for you. Bring the right tools round, like . . ."

Nora shifted a bit behind the chair and took hold of Janey's arm. Janey felt her trembling slightly.

"But I don't know you from Adam, do I?"

Reggie shrugged. "I don't know you neither. Same difference, i'n it? You might let me do you a day's work then blow me out with sixpence. I'm takin' a chance an' all, look at it like that . . ."

Nora stood there frowning between Reggie and Janey; and all at once Janey could sense her coming up to the question she definitely didn't want to hear. She even closed her eyes as if that might somehow stop it from being asked.

"What do you think, Kelly? Shall we take a chance on this young man?"

Now all the attention had shifted to Janey: who knew that she could only be a loser now, whichever way the old woman decided: because if Reggie came he'd really turn this place over for what he was after, and there'd be no more coming round here for her any more. And if he didn't, he'd just about kill her to get the money for him, like she'd promised.

Blast it! She'd thought he'd been lying a bit quiet . . .

"Well? What do you think?" Nora asked.

"Yeah, what do you think . . . Kelly?"

Janey sighed. "Yeah," she said. What else could she say? "You an' me didn't do so brilliant, did we?"

Reggie went away whistling; and with all the pleasure gone out of the day, Nora's big laugh forgotten and nothing to show for her own aching back, Janey helped to clear things up and trailed off home herself.

But as she went, something forced her to stop at the gate and take a long backward look at the window. And she had to spit in the gutter to get a nasty taste from her mouth. Something bitter. The hard-to-put-your-tongue-on taste of losing more than your money.

SIX

All that Saturday morning at Nora's Janey felt like a traitor, knowing what Reggie was up to. She did her best not to help him, tried not to give him any excuses for getting into the house, tried – without seeming to – to keep the old lady about all the time, in the way. And for a while she thought she was winning, with Reggie working hard out there playing what he thought was a waiting game, her weeding paths and Nora Woodcroft wiping down walls. It was all she'd turned up for now, the off-chance of keeping him out. Because she'd failed in the week, disappointed herself by saying nothing. She'd had her chances, they'd worked hard on their own and together, and she'd had every opportunity to level with Nora and tell her that Reggie was a thief. But she hadn't. She'd nearly done it tons of times, but when her mouth had opened for the prepared words to come out she'd suddenly turned them into something else instead. And while Nora must have thought she was daft, she knew that she was a traitor, and the feeling was something she needed like a gut full of poison. The least she could do, in the end, was turn up and try to stop anything happening. But he beat her, the so-and-so, and Janey didn't even know quite when. Perhaps it was when she went in the kitchen and gave the old lady a hand doing the cushion covers: or when they got themselves caught on the wrong side of the carpet which Janey dragged out for them both to beat. But suddenly he was standing there, with a finger on the doorbell shouting that he'd got to go, that he'd done the best he could with the old scythe his dad had lent them for nothing.

Nora followed her frame to the front door and the pair of them looked out. It was certainly better than it had been before; at least the long grass was lying flat on the top. But it still needed raking and burning, with the mower run over it finally, to call it a proper job.

"That's fifteen quid of hard graft, you got there," Reggie said. "Rest's easy."

Janey peered out from behind the old woman and saw Reggie's shirt by the front gate, a handy cover-up on the ground. He'd got something under there, she could tell, and now he was clearing off.

"Fifteen?" Nora's voice was shocked. "I hadn't bargained on fifteen."

"Eh? Listen, I've done you a favour. Call a firm in, you'd 'ave been lookin' at fifty, not miserable fifteen. Cheap labour, you've had, missus, best part o' three hours. That's five pound an hour, no tools to find an' no V.A.T. Cheap labour? Slave labour, that was, more like."

"But it isn't really done, is it?" The deep disappointment showed on Nora's face. It was clear she'd imagined a Buckingham Palace lawn by the end of the day; but even if he'd been straight as a die, Reggie could never have managed that.

"Rake up, that's all. The kid can do that. Course, I'll stay if you like. But you're running yourself into big money after twelve. Double time. Now, come on, missus, 'cos I'm in a hurry ... "

Janey could see that he was, too, hopping from one boot to the other and with every other word shooting a quick eye to his shirt by the gate. But at least he hadn't given away that they both lived in the same house ...

"Oh, all right. I suppose it's Hobson's choice, isn't it?" Nora Woodcroft reversed her frame and went to the cupboard under the stairs. She emerged with three new five pound notes.

Reggie's eyes went big; sent messages to Janey telling her they knew now where the money was. Which left Janey looking surprised. Because if it wasn't the cash Reggie had found, what was it?

"Fifteen, young man. Daylight robbery. And you needn't

come back." Nora balanced herself proudly while she thrust the money at him.

"Don' worry, I won't. Stupid ol' cow!"

The old woman slammed the door rather than watch him go: but that was only helping Reggie, because what he had to scoop up all innocently from down by the gate was a darned sight more than his shirt.

It was as if by some instinct Nora knew she had to check everything upstairs. Like knowing you're being stared-at in the back, there's a sense of knowing when trouble is in the air. It's an unease, a feeling in the pit of the stomach which can never quite be placed. But mothers have it in wartime, and like the words of her wish not coming for Janey, even without pinpointing the feeling, the meaning was there just the same.

"Upstairs," said Nora. "Come upstairs with me, lovie, please . . ."

There was an urgency in her voice, and Janey knew only too well why they had to go. She knew what was in the old woman's mind, and with a sinking feeling she knew the sort of thing they were going to find. Because she'd done it herself, hadn't she? All right, this was Nora's house, and she'd never do it here; but she'd do it next door, or over the road, or somewhere down in Plumstead. And a pound to a penny she'd be doing it again before she was much more than a couple of days older. So she knew, all right: and she also knew what Reggie was like. It was with slow, unhappy legs, then, that she followed Nora's urgent gallop up the stairs.

But there was no way she could have known the depth of the misery she would see: the terrible effect that people like Lou and Reggie and she had on people, just by being what they were.

Nora had gone straight for her own bedroom: and she'd shouted her first "Oh!" before Janey had made it to the landing window: then there'd come a low wave of whimpers while Janey rushed to the bedroom door – and had suddenly seen for the first time the destruction of a person that burglary brings.

The old woman was staring at the top of the tallboy, making pathetic movements with her hands across the bare surface. "He's gone!" she shrilled. "My Rudy! Oh no! Oh no, please, God, no!" All at once, she dropped, fell to the floor as if she didn't care whether or not she ever got up again: scrambled with her hands under the bed, under the tall-boy, into the corners, behind the curtains, made a passionate, frantic search for the trophy. "Rudy!" she cried again. "Oh, Rudy!" She moaned in her throat as she crawled and wept, as she brushed like some ineffective dog at the scattered mud off Reggie's boots. "You *bugger*!" she suddenly screamed at the thief. "You rotten little *bugger*!" In a scrabbling, crab-like move she went for her handbag on the bedside table, tipped it up to allow a couple of face-powdered photographs and a lock of blonde hair to fall out. She crushed them to her. "Thank you, God, thank you for that!" she wept. "But, oh. . . !"

Janey stared, her own face tight. This was like her nan when Grandad had died, this crying and shouting and carrying on. She watched Nora collapse from all fours and sit as she'd sat by their fire that other day, wailing and rocking and keeping on saying, "Oh, no!" At which Janey suddenly found herself going to her and hugging her. "My Rudy!" Nora moaned, and Janey could feel the misery trembling in her body. "My Rudy . . . *our* Rudy! How could he? How . . . *could* . . . he?" Her back was hot and her hair gone matted, the smell of the gardening on her and on Janey. "He's all I had. All I had of . . . what I was. Of *Nora*!" She shouted her name, loud and sudden in her unhappiness. "I'm just any old girl now . . . that's all that young bugger's left behind!"

Janey hugged her tighter. "No," she said. "No. You're still special. I know about it, don' I? You're still special to me. Eh?" And she kissed the old woman for comfort; more than a peck; a kiss on the cheek two years in the coming. And they hugged, and they rocked, getting slower and slower, until after a full half-hour, Janey finally persuaded Nora to let herself be helped up; and even got the shadow of a smile at the mention of a nice hot cup of tea.

It was little wonder Janey didn't feel much like sleep that night: she had never been so mixed-up in all her life. The house had been empty when she'd got in from Nora's, and it was empty when she went to bed: Lou had got a ticket for the bare-knuckle boxing in a factory canteen, and she could guess the sort of business Reggie was out on: but at least it left her on her own while her brain turned everything over.

She ate nothing, didn't fancy food, couldn't get into anything on the telly; and in the end she went upstairs and shut the bedroom door, sat in what passed for silence on their estate and tried to sort out the terrible mix she was in.

What about that poor old girl? Her mind kept going back to her in that other bedroom. Who'd ever have thought anyone could get so upset over something. To Nora, Reggie thieving that statue had been just like having someone die on her. She'd gone on and on, crying and trying to be brave in turns, but saying how no-one could ever bring it back. Really pathetic, it had been – and, to be honest, it had been a bit of a relief to get away.

And what about Janey Pearce? She'd suffered, too: because that was the other thing: there wouldn't be any going back, would there? Rotten Reggie had put the tin lid on that for good! With the police about to be called, she'd got away just in time: told a lie about going out with her dad. They'd have soon sussed out her name wasn't Kelly, and they'd have turned this place over from top to bottom. It would have been a right birthday for them, too, going through Lou's house: a stolen video, a school telly: and how could you say I.L.E.A. was your auntie's initials, like Reggie reckoned? They'd have known they were onto a house-full of thieves, and Janey in with them.

No, one way and another, Reggie had done it for her. He'd finished her with the old woman, and because of that, because

89

she daren't go back for her wages, he'd knocked the gymnastics on the head as well. Brilliant, wasn't it?! Nora gone, Deptford Centre gone, and soon old Mary gone, too. And of it all, the worst, she decided, as she looked down at her dirty, gardening feet, had to be losing the old woman. She'd liked all that, really enjoyed it, even all the hard work. It had seemed to be something that could last. Janey sighed, a long drawn-out breath on the back of a swear-word. It was the same as old Nora after she'd fallen over; when some people were down, especially people like Janey, they stayed down, no matter what. It seemed to be a sort of law. So perhaps the quicker she got used to the idea the less miserable she'd have to finish up . . .

But that whole evening on her own, mixed-up or not, was a godsend to Janey. Those things needed to be thought through quietly: and after a couple of nights' sleep, the Saturday and Sunday, quite a lot of things got sorted out in her head. Even Reggie, sneering at her in triumph with the trophy locked in his bedroom, played his part in helping her mind to come to grips with her problem. Not that she knew it at first. What went on was subconscious.

By Monday morning, though, like the human spirit, Janey found herself starting to bounce back. P.E. came early and she was always in her natural element in the gym. Soon she was running fast at a box, hitting the springboard, jumping and swinging her arms forward and up. Slapping her hands on the box top, she was pushing them and straddling her legs to sail straight-bodied over to the mat. At least she had this, she thought. Perhaps everyone had *something*.

Mary, her partner, hadn't needed to touch her as she saw her safely over.

"That was good, Janey. You'll get in down the gymnastics, easy. You comin' round tonight? I'm gettin' my letter today . . ."

Janey's chest heaved under her off-white tee-shirt as she watched some of the others who hadn't the guts to run and go at things. Of course she'd get in, she knew that. It was only the money.

Under the shower her shoulders relaxed as the warm water washed away more of the tension, and in a soft stream of steam she rubbed herself with council soap and began to feel better.

Lou had caught her that morning: he'd got up in time to cut her off going to school, all of a sudden desperate to get some thieving done. Nothing unusual.

"Got a few 'ouses I wanna give a spin," he'd said. "Pick you up dinner time, after you've 'ad a bit to eat ..."

"Yeah? What about my mark for the afternoon?"

"Stuff your mark! I'll give you a mark, madam, if you ain't there!"

Janey had snorted. "Yeah. All right. Don't get out your pram!"

Now, face to the shower head, she went over things again, tried to work out how she felt. She realised something must have been ticking-over in her head after that bad night, because in a weird way things definitely seemed different now. She looked down at her body. She was the same to look at, still skinny and small, nothing had changed on the outside as far as she could see. But she was different inside, there was no doubt about that: and she thought she knew why. It was something to do with old Nora.

Poor old girl, she thought. Probably still going up the wall over losing her silver statue, still crying her eyes out from having that dancing prize taken. And Janey could well understand that: she could really see what her moaning had been for. It definitely wasn't the money it was worth. No way. It was for something much more important than that. Her silver Rudy had stood for what her life had been all about; winning it must have been the best thing she'd ever done. So when Reggie had nicked it, it must have been like someone thieving a gold medal a gymnast had won at the Olympics – taking something you left your kids, a bit of special gold with your name on it. No wonder

91

the stuffing had been knocked out of her. Like she'd said, her Rudy was what had made her special.

Janey's thoughts flowed with the water. Now she could see something else as well. Wasn't that sort of thing just what *she* did? What about all the old girls and the old men who must've sat down and cried over something her and Lou had stolen? Not expensive things, but things that were special to people? Janey bowed her head under the force of the water, stared at her feet. Half Nan Pearce's things hadn't been valuable, had they? But didn't she treasure them all the same? What if someone had gone off with Grandad's penny whistle?

Janey rubbed off the soap. So why hadn't she ever thought about things like this before – like her and Lou making people feel as if the world had come to an end two or three times every week? Was it because she'd never seen the other end of it before – and when you didn't have nothing precious yourself you didn't understand? Was it because they'd always shot off quick to some dodgy dealer with their old photo-frames and never minded whose picture was in them? Was it a bit like old Nora's window: her seeing the lead in it at first instead of the picture?

She couldn't say for sure – but she knew it came down to her. To Janey Pearce. Because she was part of it, too, just as much as Lou was. And even today she was letting herself be bullied into going off and doing it all again, down a few old people's streets over Plumstead. Janey blinked her eyes in the water. Going off to spoil someone's life on some ordinary afternoon: someone having it coming who didn't know it yet!

Well, so what, then? Was she going to do anything about it? Could she even it up in some way? Had she got any guts or hadn't she?

"Have you gone off under there, Janey Pearce?" Miss Wilson, aertex and gym slip, was turning off the tap. "You'll wash yourself away down the drain!"

Janey shrugged and grabbed for her stiff square of towel. "Wouldn't matter," she said. But her step out of the shower

92

was jauntier than her words. As she dripped across the floor to make a puddle by her clothes she suddenly knew she'd made up her mind: changed it in a really big way. And that meant all sorts of things could happen from now on, she knew that, too. So it wasn't only the open window which brought a shiver to her back as she started to dry herself off.

There was one greengrocer's shop in the district that seemed to do all the trade. The fruit was firm and fresh, the vegetables pricey but good: but that wasn't really the reason for its success. It drew its customers from so far afield they sometimes took taxis: and all on account of the variety of things it sold. Shoes, shirts, jewellery, leather coats: if anything could be stolen it could be sold, so long as customer and seller could be put in touch with each other. And that's what the shop did. Whatever the boys were knocking out of warehouses and helping to fall off the backs of lorries, some of it always found its way here: and satisfied customers walked out with the week-end's greens and a few carats in their 'Fresh Fruit Daily' carrier bags. A high-class shop with a high-class fence, it had the fruit and veg neatly piled in boxed sections along each side of the shop; while down the centre shuffled the queue, waiting to be served with greengrocery by Marlene Tadds at the back of the shop, or to do business with her husband in the small room behind her.

Reggie Turner queued, trying to look interested in a mountain of foreign peas. But it was obviously not his sort of shop, this; he frowned at the pods as if what he was looking at was some sort of mystery, without a picture on a freezer packet to go by. And the thing wrapped up in Sunday's paper looked as out of place as he did, something abnormally heavy to be carried in his arms.

"That ain't no head o' celery," Mrs Tadds said, straight. "What you want?"

"I wanna see George," Reggie told her in a low voice. "Is George in?"

The woman looked at the skin-head. "I dunno. Does he know you from somewhere?"

"No, 'e don't. But tell him I know Davey Reynolds."

She folded her arms and laughed for the benefit of the shop. "Everyone knows Davey Reynolds, the old soak. I'm really gonna have to tell him." It was all loud and open as if everyone in the shop, all the neighbourhood, could be trusted not to let on to the local law what went on in there. Suddenly Mrs Tadds turned her blonde head, her ear-rings flashing, and leant her top half back through the bead curtains.

"Someone got something to show you," she said. "Davey Reynolds been dribbling off again . . ."

"Yeah?"

George Tadds must have nodded because Marlene came back and with a jerk of her head told Reggie, "All right, 'e said go in."

Reggie made a pantomime tangle of getting through the beads: but eventually, with his ear-ring freed and his head back straight, he blinked in the gloom and looked for the man.

He was in a wheelchair pulled up by the side of a desk: big and meaty above, wasted below. A low lamp burned beside him. "Yeah?" He didn't look up from counting a bundle of dockets.

"Davey Reynolds reckoned you'd be interested in this," Reggie told him. "Solid silver, 'all-mark, an' 'eavy as 'ell." He unwound the newspaper from the Valentino and put the trophy carefully into George's big hands.

" 'Tis heavy, an' all!" George up-ended it, found an eye-glass from nowhere, and started reading the hieroglyphics stamped into the base. Without changing his expression, he handed it back.

"I'll give you a fiver, knock it out as a door stop."

"Do what?" Reggie spluttered. "That's solid silver. Davey Reynolds reckons that's worth four or five 'undred quid."

"Then let Davey Reynolds give it you. If that's solid, so am I. It ain't *marked* silver plate, I'll give him that, but that's all it is.

You can feel it. It's too heavy, son. You got a great big lump o' lead in there. Lead's twice the weight of silver. Tell you what. I ain't being fair. I'll give you a fiver for the lead and a tenner for the silver. Fifteen quid, top whack."

Reggie took the trophy back, weighed it in his hands. "No, you're 'aving me over. I've only got your word for it ..."

George Tadds stared at him, hard. "I won't take offence, son. I can understand, you're disappointed. But, see, it's a trophy, right? Some dancin' competition. Now what set-up's gonna give solid silver trophies? Even years back? Blimey, the Olympic Games only gives gold *plate* ..."

"Yeah, well ..." Reggie wrapped it up again.

"Take it down the nick, 'ave it valued!"

Reggie couldn't have forced a laugh if there'd been the original five hundred in it. "Yeah, anyway, ta ..." He clutched the Valentino back under his arm, threw back the beads and side-walked out of the narrow shop.

"Come again!" Marlene called after his scowl. "Looks like 'e didn't like the price o' cabbage!" she said, and a line-full of shoppers laughed with her.

The taxi carrying Ruth and Sammy Seymore from the station turned into Delaport Road, down from the bus route. The driver looked about him as if he were entering a strange land.

"Not been down here for ages," he called back as they passed the big houses. "Didn't know there was so many of them left. They're offering fortunes to buy up this sort of thing, making 'em into flats."

"Really?" said Ruth. "Round here?"

"Yeah, big development area, this is. Give me one of these to sell and you won't find me cabbing for long ..."

Sammy soured her face. "What a slum," she said. "Real *down-town*!"

Ruth looked no happier. "It's certainly changed a lot, even in a few years. I guess I never knew the council estate was so close."

"Well, they've chopped the trees down, 'aven't they? Now people can see each other – as if they ever wanted to!"

Sammy shivered. "Ugh!" she said. "How awful!"

Further down the road, through the gap in her front hedge, Nora saw the black cab coming, fixed her eyes on the two women in the back and could hardly believe that one of them was her granddaughter. But the real eyes were for Ruth. Her Ruth. And they lit and shone as mother and daughter at last came within focusing distance of each other. Nora stood balanced by the gate and tried not to cry as the confusion of arrival spread all over the pavement – bodies, holdalls, cases, kisses. The cab driver sat tight, watching it, left the women to do it all and leant over only so far as he had to to take his fare. Ruth gave him a ten pence tip. "You'd have had more if you'd helped with the bags," she told him.

" 'Ow long you been away, missus? It ain't safe to leave this seat, not any more." He looked at the house with its big stained glass window. "But I'll give *you* a decent tip. Tell her to sell. She's sitting on a gold mine there."

With a clatter the diesel drove off and the celebration spread itself nearer to the gate.

"Ruth!"

"Mother!"

"And Sammy!"

"Hi, Gran!"

"Well, *haven't* you grown?"

"Eats us out of existence!"

"Did you get some sleep on the plane?"

"Oh, Mother, do you ever? Cat-naps, that's all . . . "

Gradually they moved from the street and into the garden – luggage, walking frame, tired legs – all in one-step moves like pawns in a game of chess.

"Now give me your arm, Mother. Sammy can carry your appliance."

Nora shrugged off the help.

"Heavens, no, Ruth, I can manage on my own a treat." And

96

with her hands shaking at her first big test she turned the frame and started to walk the uneven garden path. She knew that two pairs of eyes were behind her, and she knew that what they were judging was not just whether she could make it to the door but whether or not she was fit to live on her own any more. All right, then! she suddenly thought. Go on and judge! I wasn't born yesterday: I'm not new to a bit of pressure, to having the lime-light on me, not by a long chalk! And she willed herself to think of it as a competition, the sort of thing she'd done at the Alexandra Palace, at the Kensington Town Hall, at the Lyceum – as something that she could *win*. Only now the frame was her partner again instead of Alfred, and the music was something she was having to recall. She took a deep breath, held up her head and went for the door. Her Valentino had gone, and she'd never win another silver trophy in her life: so the prize right now was more important than it had ever been. Today's prize was as big as life itself: simply being *her*.

"She's let the garden go," Ruth hissed as they followed, lugging at the cases. "It used to be her pride and joy, out here."

Sammy shivered once again. "Whole place gives me the creeps," she said, looking around at the waving trees and up at the front of the house. "Specially that spooky old window."

By now Nora was at the front door, had turned and was beaming at them. "See?" she said. "It's no more than having a stick, really. Lots of people have sticks. I'm right as rain on my frame: right as ninepence." She left time for a reply but Ruth didn't make one, kept her face very non-committal instead. "Come in, then, come in. You know where everything is, your old home's just the same, I'm not one for a lot of chopping and changing. Bathroom's where it always was. You must be really ready for a nice bath, then I've got something special for your tea ..."

Sammy pushed through and sniffed, wrinkling her nose.

"How's my treasure?" asked Nora, with an arm round her shoulder.

"O.K., I guess. Pooped."

Sammy sighed, and everyone stood silent for a moment. In which Nora suddenly made up her mind to say nothing about the Valentino being stolen, not yet. She'd meant to: but it wasn't as if things were going too well up to now. She could sense her daughter's disappointment at her frame. If on top of all her other doubts Ruth thought she was in danger from thugs and thieves, she'd have a bigger fight on her hands than she'd got already. The policeman had told her she shouldn't be living on her own: he'd agreed with Miss Stephenson. It only needed them all to get together and she'd be really outnumbered.

"Come on," she said. "My home is your home." And she wondered if Ruth would remember. But she didn't say a word: she was far too busy running her eyes around the house.

They were washing up when Janey got there. At least, Ruth was, because she refused to let Nora lift a finger; while Sammy sat and yawned as the talk went round and round. There was a lot to be said, after all: Nora and Ruth had a few years to catch up on.

While by contrast, Janey, in coming was throwing off a few years. Because she'd made the big decision and hadn't met Lou from school after dinner. She'd done what she'd thought she would and blown him out instead. Under that shower she'd made up her mind. If he wanted to go on thieving the way he did, that was down to him; but he definitely wasn't going to drag her along with him any more. From now on he could do his own knocking on the front doors, he could pretend he was collecting for his own jumble sales or a rag-and-bone round. And if he didn't like it, she'd told the classroom ceiling, he could lump it! And let him lay one finger on her and she'd be off down the nick so fast he wouldn't have time to put his hand back in his pocket before the Old Bill turned up to tear his place apart. God, she thought, she could get him put away for years if she wanted! And if she'd still had Nan Pearce to go to that's just what she would have done. A big decision – but one which meant she could afford to think about herself for a change: at least as far as getting in down at Deptford. And to follow it through she needed the wages Nora owed her, even if she couldn't afford to hang about there too long. Yes, Deptford she wanted: while Borstal she definitely didn't fancy: but as long as there wasn't a panda car outside she'd knock for the money and go.

Sammy answered the door: threw it open the way she did at home, as if it had to be some sort of unwelcome interruption. "Yeah?" She stared at Janey: pink velvet tracksuit looking at stained grey blouse. "You collecting for something?"

"No, I ain't, I've come to see the old lady; old Nora."

With a whistle, Sammy looked down the hallway behind her and came back again, an I-can't-believe-it look on her face. "You mean, you *know* her. She knows *you*?"

" 'S'right. And I know you. You're S'mantha, ain't you?" Janey was pleased to surprise her. She didn't like being looked at as if she was something the cat had brought in.

"You better wait here," Sammy said. "I'll go see if she wants to see you. You got a name?"

"Kelly."

"*Kelly*." Sammy said it with a twangy TV voice as if it were a popular brand of dog food. "Wait here."

She shut the door in Janey's face and went off down the hall. Suddenly Janey shivered as a dusty breeze swirled in the porch. It was getting cold now: and all at once things didn't seem such a good idea after all. But she needed the money, she told herself. At least a tenner: that was the only reason she'd come: that was why she was risking being asked about the silver man, taking a chance on being tarred with the same brush as Reggie. She needed the money to show willing at the Deptford Centre, to keep in with Mary – so she'd better go through with it.

But there was still an awkward ten minutes to come in the kitchen: for her and for Nora. Throwing together different sides of people's lives can lead to some painful collisions. And Janey guessed how it might be for the old woman, she knew the score, so all she could do was stand stiffly inside the door listening to

Nora singing her praises while the other two looked at her as if the old woman was mental with her nervous, over-the-top talk: Ruth all fidgety to do something else and Samantha smirking up and down, up and down, at Janey's clothes. And feeling the red in her face, Janey prayed for the payment bit to come so that she could get away without saying something to spoil things.

"She sounds like a real Good Samaritan," Sammy sang out from a stool by the dresser, with a face which still said *Pharisee*.

"Oh, she was, she is," said Nora. "I don't know what . . ." But her voice ran out suddenly, as if she'd just thought better of the wisdom of going on about the special hard work they'd both put in.

"How much does my mother owe you?" Ruth Seymore asked, cutting through it all. "Only we've got so much to do, Mother."

Janey could see Nora thinking, puzzling what to say: and suddenly she could see the problem as if it were up there in lights on the old woman's forehead. If what she owed the girl sounded a lot, she'd seem a stupid old woman who couldn't manage things properly. But if it came out too little, Kelly would think she was mean.

Ruth had produced a neat bill-fold of new money and was staring at her dithering mother.

Janey looked at Nora, saw the strain on her face, the puffy eyes where she'd cried over the statue. She remembered the hugging and the rocking in the bedroom and what the old girl had already lost. She sighed, and suddenly she let her off the hook. "Couple o' quid, that's all," she jumped in. "I like coming . . ."

Without question the money was pushed at her. Who needs enemies when I've got me? Janey asked herself as soon as she'd got it, next-to-nothing to grip in her hand. But a look at Nora's face told her that the old girl understood, she was grateful, Janey had done the right thing. Thanks, lovie. I'll make it up to you, she was winking and nodding. You see if I don't . . .

"Yeah, well, ta." It was an awkward moment, all quiet, with just the sound of shoes on the tiles. Janey coughed and turned to go. It just needed a last word to round it all off, to get her out and back down the hall: something to leave them knowing how much she cared about the old woman, how she was a friend. Putting her head on one side, she pulled a sympathetic face and said to Nora: "An' I'm sorry your nice silver dancer got took ..."

She might as well have rolled a hand grenade across the floor.

"The Valentino!" exploded Ruth. "Don't say Rudy's been stolen!"

Janey could have cut her tongue out, poor old Nora looked so distressed.

"I've told the police," Nora stuttered. "They're keeping a good eye open."

"Huh! Road blocks on the highway!" Sammy snorted.

"But he's priceless," thrust Ruth. "How could you let that happen and then say nothing about it? That's the worst family thing I've heard since cousin Jimmy died. Dad must be turning in his grave!"

Nora was crying. "It's a *thing*, not a *person*," she said. "People are what matter, not objects. And you're healthy, I'm all right, Sammy's ... let's be grateful for all of that ..."

But Ruth hadn't finished. This was all ammunition, her face said, ammunition in the battle to consolidate the fact that her mother couldn't cope. She drew in another breath – and Janey decided to go. Not that anyone noticed. Everything was in such turmoil in the kitchen she could have lit a fire in the hall without anyone caring. But before the door banged she heard Sammy going on about 'poor-house kids': and she broke into a run in case they suddenly wanted her back.

She screwed up the paltry two pounds in her hand. What a rotten turn-out! No money, no job, no gymnastics. And now, on top of all that, the time had come to go home and face up to Lou. She'd imagined doing it with something to cheer about going on secretly inside, nice feelings from going straight, good times at the Deptford Club to look forward to with Mary. When you've got something else to turn to you can get through some

101

really rough patches. But now there was *nothing*: and the stupid thing was, she'd only got her softness to blame.

She turned the corner and there was Lou, face like thunder, staring down the street for her.

"Where the 'ell was you? I sat there like a right berk for 'alf hour outside that school!" He was snorting angry and his big hands were twitching at his belt. "Eh?" She went in and he suddenly slammed the front door shut behind her to cut off any hope of a quick escape. "Eh?" he shouted, thrusting his big face at her.

Janey looked up at it, searched it for the slightest sign of something kind. But there wasn't one: nothing in the eyes, nothing in the mouth. When he got in a mood like this Lou could be a real bully, and you could forget how easily he could be twisted the rest of the time.

"Well?" He slapped her round the head. "*Where was you?*"

Janey's ear rang. The blow was hard enough to make her stagger to regain her balance. It didn't hurt but it would in a minute, and there was more where that came from, she could tell. It definitely wasn't a time to stand up to him. If she told him she was finished with thieving she'd have to have room to run, and somewhere to go.

"Ouch! Hold on! They saw me. Ol' Miss Welton. They wouldn't let me out. Go and slap *them* round the 'ead."

"They wouldn't let you out? What you on about? Did you tell 'em your father wanted you out?"

"Yeah."

"An' they wouldn't let you? I'm bleedin' comin' up that school! They got no right to go against me!"

He slapped his hand smack on the wall. But at least it wasn't Janey's head.

"I told 'em that. They said you hadn't wrote a letter."

"I'll give 'em a letter! I'll throw the bloody book at 'em! I'll ... How bloody *dare* they?"

But he was taking his temper out on the banister rail as well now, and then on the kitchen door which he slammed with

102

enough force to set the light bulb swinging. And Janey, diving into the front room, clutching at her ear, guessed she might have accidentally found the answer. Perhaps if she said they were watching her at school, he might start dropping her out of his plans for himself. He'd never start writing letters to the school to get her out in the afternoons because he knew they kept those, and could check on her, send the attendance woman round, that sort of thing – and that definitely wouldn't suit him. The video flashed up another green minute. In the street outside some kids argued the toss. In the kitchen the fridge door slammed as Lou pulled out a beer. Depressed, Janey looked out of the dirty window. The same old view. And nothing to change it now. Nowhere to go, not even for an evening. No gymnastics – and she daren't show her face back at the old lady's, not any more. She'd probably die looking out at this view, she thought, when she was an old girl herself.

Another video click.

And look at that window. Janey put her head on one side, touched the glass with a trembling hand. Weird, wasn't it, how this bit of glass and that brilliant coloured picture both went by the same name? *Window*. Different as chalk and cheese, but both called the same. She shrugged, and her hand went back to the heat of her ear. Like people, she decided. All called people but look at that Samantha, and look at her. No-one giving a toss for Janey, and Samantha with everyone running round and she couldn't care less.

She stood, and stared, and the bare window slowly began watering into a blur. With a sleeve Janey vigorously wiped at her eyes. She didn't cry. So what was this? Christ, was she going soft all over today?

Reggie wrenched her out of her mood. With a bang he was in the street door, a short string of obscenities and he was in the front room. Twisted in aggression, he looked as if he might throw the thing in his hand at the television. But suddenly he spat at the electric bar and hurled the Valentino

103

trophy into the corner of the settee. The spit flashed up a blue
spark: the trophy kicked up dust and bits of crisps.

"Useless! That divvock, Davey Reynolds! Made me look a
right berk, didn't 'e? Wait 'till I get 'old of 'im!"

Janey wasn't sure whether it was safe to ask what was up
with the statue.

"*Plated*, i'n it? 'Ardly buy me a tank o' petrol let alone a
motor-bike! An' I'm in there with the man like some village
idiot. Lost all me street cred!"

Janey drew back, got a hand to a cushion, waited for him to
turn it all on her. But he didn't. As suddenly as he'd come in he
slammed out of the room. By some miracle he was going to take
it out on someone else instead.

"The movement'll soon sort him!" Reggie thumped up the
stairs. "'E don't make an idiot out o' one of us!"

Janey even smiled. No need to, she thought, you're idiots
enough already. She picked up the Valentino from its nose-dive
into the settee, stood it on its feet against the wall and switched
on the television. But she couldn't lose herself, couldn't quieten
her thoughts, and after half an hour of fidgeting she took herself
out to the kitchen to eat whatever she could lay her hands on.
When there was nothing else going for you, at least you could
get a bit of comfort from a mouthful or two of food.

SEVEN

Mary didn't often come up onto the estate. Janey rarely expected to be called for, and never before school. She was having a wash the next morning when she heard the front door slam and before she knew it Reggie had come kicking into the bathroom.

"There's some wog askin' for you," he told her. "Outside." He said it with that skin-head hatred which looks a lot like diseased gums.

Janey dressed herself quickly and ran out of the house. She loathed Reggie for being skin-head, sneered at his pathetic badges and his twisted brain, but all the same it was more than her life was worth to ask Mary in. It'd all be too painful to think about. Mary was hanging on the gate and even Reggie's Ku-Klux door-slam didn't seem to have wiped the smile right off her face. She had a letter in a long white envelope, and by the crumpled looks of it, it had been read a million times that morning.

"I got me letter, Janey." She was jumping on the pavement. "I passed the test, they're lettin' me join."

"Oh, that's all right, then." Janey didn't even want to sound pleased, because she wasn't. Being honest, she'd have done the jumping herself if Mary had failed.

"They said I got a high over-all standard. Look."

Mary pushed the paper into Janey's hand, who read it as they walked along, nodding her way down through the letter. "It's good!" Till she came to the final paragraph. She stopped nodding then. "'Ere, what's this?"

Mary had floated on, had to come back. "Oh, yeah, I was gonna tell you . . ." She kicked her shoes against a wall while Janey read aloud:

"*Due to a high demand for places, members who have been accepted must enrol by Friday, 17th October with the first term's fees fully paid. The first club night will be on Wednesday, 22nd October at 7 p.m., for which full kit (see list) is essential.*"

"Yeah, I saw that ..."

"But they're saying I'm too late already."

"No...?" Mary looked over Janey's shoulder. "Didn't notice the dates. Ain't you got enough money for the test? Can't you go Wednesday or something? Still gives you two days till Friday, don't it?"

The letter cracked in the air as Janey handed it back. "Listen, I could pass top mark an' I still wouldn't have that sort o' money by Friday," she said. "It's not worth even talking about no more, right?"

Mary shrugged. "O.K." She pulled a face. "Sorry. Wouldn't have come round bein' all pleased if I'd known that ..."

But Janey couldn't find the words to make it all right: and she didn't even want to. All she wanted to do was what she was doing: walking on along the pavement and cursing the whole rotten world.

Sammy's day had started badly too. At eight o'clock her shoulder had been shaken and her bedclothes thrown back to her feet.

"Hey! What's going on here?"

It was her mother, already up and dressed and wearing a business look on her face.

"It's the only way to beat jet-lag, Sammy; Daddy told me. You get up and force yourself through the day, it gets you into the proper sleeping pattern for England. Two or three nights and you'll be fine."

Sammy tried to retrieve the sheets. "I'm fine right now. I'm staying here!"

But Ruth had other ideas. "Come on, I've told your grand-mother you're getting up and up you're getting!" She pulled

Sammy's legs round to force her out onto the floor. "Hurry now, I want you to run to the store. There's a whole bag-full of cleaning stuff I want."

Sammy yawned, and shivered. "Call the store on the telephone, why don't you? Have them send the stuff round."

But Ruth was halfway to making the bed again. "They don't deliver in England. And stop making a fuss: you can be heard! You know I shan't sit down till I've been through this place with Dettol and Breeze." She sniffed at her old room, looked up to where the cobwebs were maypoling round the light flex. "There's a year's work to do in a week in this house – quite apart from making arrangements. So shift yourself, young lady, or I'll start losing patience."

"You have to have it to lose it!" Sammy shouted. And the bathroom lock just saved her from a good slap.

Janey saw her coming up the street. It cheered her a bit. What a show-up! she thought.

"'Ere, Mare, look what's fell out the fancy-dress parade!" She nodded down the pavement at the sight of Sammy coming towards them in full tennis gear: light-blue tracksuit top, big Elton John sunglasses and a large nylon shopping bag in her hand.

Mary screeched. "Don't mind dreamin', but *stuff* a nightmare! Who *is* she?"

"That's the new kid where I done that work. Comes from Canada."

"Canada? Long way to get your shopping, i'n it?"

Janey laughed: but it really made her feel sad. All this would stop when they went their different ways.

For a moment she wondered if she should lose herself, not run the risk of what the Canadian might call her. But Sammy was coming and her expression said how certain it was she wasn't going to speak.

"Talk about *honky*, Janey!"

All eyes, but with mouths tight shut, Janey and Sammy passed, neither of them needing to pull a face to show the way they felt. Janey thought the other girl might have sniffed, but she didn't make anything of it.

"Wouldn't mind them trainers," Mary said. "They're Dunlop 'Professionals'."

"I wouldn't mind any of it," said Janey, thinking along different lines. "'Cept her mum. Nothing's got to be worth that one . . ."

The interlude over, in silence they walked on to school. Inside the school gate two girls were waiting for Mary, each with a long, white envelope in their hands and with faces as bright as Broadway. By the time the palm slapping and the congratulations had died down, Janey had muttered a quiet "See you," and wandered off to go and lean against the wall of the lavatory. But walking past Samantha had bugged her as well. That kid had seen her with Mary: and Mary was wearing her school uniform. Even from behind those dark glasses she'd be able to see the badge, and from that anyone'd know what school she went to. Which was one more way of finding out who Janey really was.

She shrugged. So what! If the police came and found her, if they asked her where she lived and searched her house, if they found the silver statue and locked up Lou and Reggie, so what? She'd get put into care somewhere, that's all! A good bit better, that might be, than the way things were going right now.

She swore at a kid who'd kicked his ball too near her head. "You can belt-up flea-bag!" he shouted. Janey let him go. She'd been scruffy so long she hardly heard the word any more.

Care. Now that didn't sound too bad at that. Being taken into *care*. It was a word with a good sound to it, a bit like *warm* and *comfort*. The kids who came in from care in a transit every day didn't seem to mind. But to be fair she didn't know any of them very well. And, she had to face it, people always picked words to make things sound good, didn't they? Like 'benefit'.

She itched a shoulder-blade on the brick. She looked across the yard and saw Mary describing her gym test with her hands in the air. That lot were all so high it wasn't true.

But, no, it definitely wasn't Lou and Reggie and the care thing which worried her about being found. Down inside, she knew it was something else, another reason for not wanting the police up at the school. It was the old woman, old Nora. She'd liked Kelly; she'd said so, and she'd acted like it, too. Apart from Mary she'd been the only person since her nan who'd ever had time for her, felt like that about her, really taken to her. Hadn't she said Janey was her sort, been over the moon because she'd known a couple of the old sayings? Hadn't she liked her enough to want her to come three times a week to see her? And not just to do jobs, either, but to sit in the kitchen and drink tea and lemonade and be a bit of company. And what about those crackers, and the fire, and the hugs and the kisses? Something a bit special, all that had been. No, the police coming up would mean she'd blown all that in the old girl's mind. Kelly not going back she'd put down to those other two being there: but if she was definitely sussed, what rotten thoughts would go through old Nora's mind then? Janey turned and faced the wall, picked at a brick while her stomach rolled. She was probably thinking them anyway, whether the law came up or not! That family wasn't stupid. They probably knew, had her for a con artist. She swallowed: that was a very hard lump to get down, that was.

But she'd got one thing going for her, Janey told herself. She'd never been the sort to give in easy. When the back door was locked she looked in the window: even took a chance and went round the front. At the first bit of a drawback she didn't give in, she found other ways. So wasn't there some way she could put things straight between her and the old lady? Just let her know, and leave it? What about...? Even if she had to drop the word about Reggie, couldn't she make sure Nora knew how Janey Pearce could be trusted – how she wasn't just your run-of-the-mill little toe-rag like Lou always made out?

The bell went and people started drifting off towards their different doors. But Janey didn't move: she looked up from under the shadow of her own bent head and watched Mary splitting from the others and pushing her way towards her. Good old Mare, she couldn't keep it up for ever, but at least she was trying to be all right.

"Comin' in? What we got first lesson?"

Janey shook her head. "Dunno," she said. "Maths, weren't it?" She took a step forward, but in the same movement turned back, walked in a tight, moody circle. "I ain't comin'. Just remembered. I got a job to do."

"A job? What you on about, missus? Not another bank?"

But already Janey was moving off against the tide, sliding through the waves of navy blue. "See you, Mare," she called. And while Mary watched, she disappeared from view and took the course she'd just at that moment plotted in her head.

The Valentino was exactly where she'd left it, still standing at a tilt on the ruck of the carpet behind the settee. And Reggie was out, with Lou still dead to the world in bed. She picked up the trophy, the sleek-haired, silver dancing man, and put him gently into an old plastic bag, so heavy he had to be laid flat along the bottom like a bottle of drink from the off-licence. Clutching him she hurried out of the house and headed for Delaport Road, light and fast now, because she knew exactly what she was going to do and what she was going to say.

She was going to march up to old Nora's front door, take no notice of the kid who opened it, and insist on seeing the old lady – on her own. She'd call out down the hall if need be. Then, in the front room or somewhere, she'd give her back the silver man and she'd tell her where she'd found it: chucked under a big rubbish bin over by the flats, where someone – the gardening boy probably – had thought it'd be safe till people stopped looking. "There's always a load of talk," she'd say, "someone always knows something up the estate . . . " And if she *could* get

110

the old girl on her own it'd wear, she knew that. She wasn't the sort to be too suspicious of a good story. Quite the reverse – she'd meet Kelly half-way, she knew that. In any case she'd be feeling bad about owing her money, and hadn't she spent ten minutes telling the others what a treasure Kelly was? No, she'd be all right, Janey reckoned, if only she could get in to see her. Then at least they'd be straight. Because what she also knew, deep down, was that it definitely wasn't the money she was after any more. She might get it or she might not. Be nice to have it, no sense kidding herself, but she'd gone past the gymnastics things now. This was just to get the silver statue back to her, to put it all right, to leave old Nora thinking those nice things about her that she'd thought when they'd sat by the fire. Whatever happened, whether she ever went there again or not, she didn't want Nora thinking the worst of her. She wasn't a toe-rag, she was going straight now, and she was all old Nora had thought she was. A kind and loving girl. And somehow, having the old woman keeping on thinking that was as important as anything had been for a long time.

Hurrying now, Janey came through the estate and turned into Delaport Road. The sun was getting up and was just about warm enough to keep her the right side of feeling chilly. Out of the breeze she could almost think it was still summer: especially, all of a sudden, hearing the plonk of a tennis ball somewhere near. No, it wasn't her imagination; and being a sound out of its time, within a few steps it had forced her to stop. Sure enough, a real ball was being banged about with all the rhythm of a Wimbledon knock-up: no voices: no kids arguing the toss: just a ball, tight strings, and a wall. Who was that, then, down here by the bulldozed houses?

It was Sammy: on an old garage base with a cleared space, practising her returns from off the wall with all the concentration of Centre Court. Janey saw her from the pavement, before she was spotted herself. She wasn't all that good, she thought. For someone with all the gear like she had, all the clothes and the bat and the wired-up teeth, she was all sorts of rubbish, really. Given half a chance Janey could have beaten her hollow using the tatty old stuff from school. With a sneery sort of smile on her face, waiting to be seen grinning really wide at some bad mistake, Janey leant at the end of the wall and watched her. The little snurd really reckoned herself, she thought. She had all the habits: hitching her tracksuit off her back even though it was no way cold enough to sweat: grunting when she served, although her service didn't have the strength of a school dinner jelly: and then the big show-up – stopping to tick off a make-believe photographer at the side of the court – "Damn camera clicks! Do you have to throw my concentration?"

That was the moment to cough and come out. "You winning yourself, are you?" Janey asked.

Sammy looked as if a door had just been opened on her. "Hell, who're you creeping up on?"

"Not a lot, by the looks of it!"

"You give me a pain, you know that?"

"That's more'n you give that ball ..."

"Oh, yeah?"

The atmosphere had suddenly changed: it was that moment when traffic noises stop and birds leave off singing. Janey put down the bag on the concrete base in case she needed her hands. She had a strong feeling she would. The two girls stared at one another, a hostile gulf between them even wider than the Atlantic Ocean. Janey could see Sammy weighing up whether to make some move with the racquet. And suddenly she did: but it was only to start bouncing her ball on it.

"I wasn't practising brute force," she said. "I'm doing accuracy training today."

"Yeah? You wasn't even gettin' 'em over the net!"

"I was, too! I've got that net right here in my eye."

"What, with them flash guns goin' off?" Janey mocked. "I've definitely got to get a paper in the morning, see if they've put you in it! Yeah – the *Daily Wallie*, I'll get."

Fifty dollars of Dunlop came at her. With the ball still in the air, Sammy wristed the handgrip round and sliced the racquet at Janey. "You tramp!" she shouted. Janey saw it coming and jumped, but the shot was good this time and the head spun through the air and caught her a painful blow on the hip.

"Ow! You cow!" And in a leaping reflex she went straight for Sammy's head, grabbing hold of a handful of hair and swinging her round on her heel. With a left she punched at her face, while the other girl, shrieking, grabbed back at Janey, got a grip of her curls and fell off-balance with her weight underneath. Down Janey went, the other one with her, locked like lobsters and kneeing and kicking, pulling at each other's heads with both their hands. It was a fist of Janey's hair that was torn away first: she felt it go, swore and forgot it as she caught the other off-balance, bit at an arm and put in a knee to take advantage of being on top. But Sammy squirmed and pulled free, got to the hair again and jabbed her own sharp knee-cap into Janey. Janey swore, kicked and pulled, tried all the street tricks she knew. But she was up against a good fighter: there was nothing la-di-da about the way the Canadian butted and bit back, jacked her knee again and again in a painful jerking of blows. Kids who knew Janey gave up before she really started but this one didn't know her and she kept going like a wild cat in a corner. Elbows got split, knees started bleeding, heads were yanked this side and that as the hair came out. One was on top, then the other. Too evenly matched, it had to be a fight to a bloody finish: another knee jacking in, the warm run of blood from a torn ear, for a fraction Janey letting go just a bit, a push and a roll and Sammy on top again, scratching her nails at Janey's face. One desperate shove back and they thrashed over once more, all hands, arms, legs, teeth; panting, swearing, bleeding; with the torn hair flying like floss in swirlings of dust. Seeing a wild chance Janey pulled herself off, dragged in a breath to come crashing down: but Sammy's legs swung on through thin air and clattered into the bag by the wall. With a dull clang it flapped over – and out rolled the Valentino trophy: shining on the concrete in the grey morning light.

Both the girls froze; but guilt held Janey still for a second too long. Samantha grabbed at the dancer and leapt to her feet, eyes all alight, fingers pointing.

"*You* snatched it! You cheap little cheat! *You* snatched it!"

"I never."

"*Wonderful Kelly! Marvellous Kelly!*"

"It weren't me!"

"Snatched it, now you're going to town to sell it!"

"I ain't!" Janey picked herself up. "I ain't! If you must know, I'm bringing it back!"

"My ass! Kelly the thief!" Sammy's face suddenly lit with real triumph. "Or how about *Janey the cheat*? Eh? *Janey*?"

Janey's mouth filled with blood.

"Anyhow, I don't care which you are, you don't fool me!" And Sammy turned and ran: left her racquet where it had fallen and, cradling the Valentino like a baby, took off fast down the street towards Nora's.

Janey spat the blood from her mouth and swore. Oh, Christ! That was it, then! That really was the end! The little creep had heard Mary going on, hadn't she, walking down the street, calling her Janey? A big tin lid again! That was definitely the finish – getting caught with the silver thing before she could give it back, found out pulling a con with her name. Old Nora would have to be out of her mind to believe what she said now!

Hurting more inside than out, she looked back up the street where she had to go: back the way she'd come: back to Lou, and back to Reggie who'd have missed the silver man – and all without a kind word from Nora to help hold up her head.

It had all gone so wrong it wasn't true!

Janey looked at the concrete where they'd fought. Hair, the other's blonde and her own black, was blowing round in circles. In swift, stopping movements she scooped hers up, a whole thick handful of it, and pushed it down into the plastic bag. No-one was finding that. She wasn't leaving that to blow around in the street. No-one was gloating over bits of Janey Pearce.

114

She walked off home, eyes on her shoes. But it wasn't really the hair, she thought miserably, hair would grow again. It was for something else down that road she was feeling a sharp sense of loss. Old Nora's smile and her clapping hands when she was happy: her trust and the way she'd talked to her: the cuddle she gave you like Nan Pearce. And all that, Janey suddenly knew, having tasted it and liked it, was something she was really going to miss.

PART TWO

SPRING INTO SUMMER

EIGHT

Like a council crocus Janey came through the winter only
because the town hall cared. School meals, a warm classroom
and a clothing grant kept her going when Lou had become
useless, and her show in the spring was thanks to rates and
committees, not to any digging her stepfather did at home.
They were hard months: tough: school with Mary making her
plans with other people now, home with Reggie more and more
into skin-head stuff and beatings up, trying to involve her in his
schemes to get even with hated enemies like Kipper. And of the
two, home was a hundred times worse. Reggie threatened her
sometimes when she said no to his plans, and more than once
she spent a cold evening out till late, preferring to freeze than to
face him before he'd got high and fallen asleep. And she had one
big upset with Lou. He'd been on the beer with money he'd got
off someone: three days it had lasted, and three days it had
taken him to get over it: but when he was more or less dried out,
with only the stale malty smell of a binge about him, he came
over restless and wanted to get back to thieving. On the fourth
afternoon he went out on his own, but two hours later he came
back with nothing, having had a close shave and almost got
caught. The next day it was clear he was determined to get his
confidence back, or bust. He was jumpy all over the place and
he kept at Janey to go out with him again. He suggested, he
pleaded and he bullied: and hard as she tried, she didn't have
the resistance to say no. It fell in the January before the schools
went back and she couldn't hold the Welfare over him, not for
making her miss lessons. Besides which, for the first time in
earnest, he started to unbuckle that big belt of his. So Janey
went out with him and genuinely did her best. Lou had found a
big hotel on Blackheath with the 'For Sale' sign up, a Georgian

building being converted into thirty small flats: and from the talk in a local pub he'd discovered that prior to phase two beginning, an old Irish housekeeper was holding the fort and sitting on a pile of rich pickings from the rooms: things like ripped-out marble tops and disconnected televisions, not to mention a fortune in drink from the cellar. All he needed was for Janey to knock and check that the woman was out when he'd heard she would be.

One Saturday lunchtime Janey stood on the front step of the hotel and pulled at a bell for ages. She rang and she rang and she bossed through the letter-box; and there was nothing, all the expected signs of the old Irishwoman being off sipping gin down the road. But the minute Janey gave the all clear to Lou to back-in the van, round came the woman from out in the garden, demanding to know which bloody contractor he worked for, turning up on a Saturday! Janey got a good clout from Lou that day. But while the stings were still on her, she yelled back at him, "Don't never ask me no more!" And he didn't. After a day or two of cursing her he slumped back into borrowing from one woman or another, and whenever talk of thieving came up, Janey looked the other way.

So she went on, just about existing, very, very depressed. Having seen another way of life in the autumn; more, almost having it for herself and then losing it through really bad luck, probably made it worse. But during the cold months she fell so low in her mind that if she'd been an adult she'd have had some sort of clinic treatment: whereas being a kid, the school simply called her sullen and her form tutor said she was 'going through that difficult stage'. Physically she grew a bit: but mentally she shrivelled, she lost her rough diamond shine, and for Janey Pearce the spring when it pushed through didn't arrive a day too soon.

But a walk, one morning, down a sheltered street with the sun coming out of the blue to lay warm across her shoulders, and Janey suddenly had the slightest feel of better days: a blackbird singing somewhere in a garden sounded like summer: and something in Janey rose to this faintest voice of hope.

"Clear off, Bennett!" she shouted at a boy who'd been getting away with murder all winter: she swung her bag and caught him a nasty one. "I ain't tellin' you again!"

With a lift in her step she went in to find that school was different, too. Teachers were sending round for window poles to let some air in and the time was all over the place after the clocks had gone forward. School dinners had a few salads on offer and a jam sandwich went through the sunshine roof of the headmaster's car. All at once there was something to smile at.

But what really made the day special, lifted it up from any other change of season in school, was what came in a lesson Janey usually loathed, in Religious Education on the north side of the building where the sun hardly ever got round the corner. Miss Fairweather, all street talk and posh voice, told them to open their books and read round the class from page ninety-eight.

"Now, this story's all about voting with your feet," she said to those who were listening, Janey still yawning, Mary writing a note. "This story's about not blowing town to do your own thing, but putting up with *zilch*, all out of loyalty." And what a shock to find, when Janey came-to and turned over a few pages, that Miss Fairweather was actually on about something she'd heard of before – the story of Ruth, the same story as that old lady's window. It gave her a funny feeling to come across it again, as if she sort of owned it, and in her seat at the window, warmed by the sun and by a couple of thoughts of old Nora, Janey read her piece when her turn came with a weird sense of coming back from being somewhere else. Her reading came from near the bottom of the page, and the words came out very familiar: *'You see,' said Naomi, 'your sister-in-law has gone back to her people and her gods; go back with her.' 'Do not urge me to go back and desert you,' Ruth answered. 'Where you go, I will go, and where you stay, I will stay. Your people shall be my people, and your God my God. Where you die, I will die, and there I will be buried. I*

121

swear a solemn oath before the Lord your God: nothing but death shall divide us.'

Miss Fairweather shouted for another reader to take over and Janey stopped. Stopped reading, but her mind was going on, was filled with old Nora and her window, with thoughts about that story, with the fire they'd had and the wish she couldn't think of, with how nice it had nearly been: the sort of thoughts which run on and on in the right mood to where anything suddenly seems possible. Janey even found herself imagining being that Ruth, caught a quick glimpse of herself winning through. And didn't she deserve it? her eyes asked out of the window. All right, she might not have been bent double all winter in the fields; but her winter in Woolwich hadn't exactly been anything to shout about, had it?

So what, she wondered even more wildly, if she bent over backwards to do something which took almost as much guts? *What if she went to the old girl to explain to her everything that had happened?* All of the truth? It was a crazy thought. It would mean taking a really big chance, running the risk of having the door slammed in her face and being treated like a crook: but what if she actually went to see her? *Honesty is always the best policy*, Nan Pearce used to say. A million miles from Lou's sort of advice, and she'd be turning in her grave over the way things were now. But it just might be true. Besides, those Canadians, they wouldn't still be there, would they? Plus the police would be well out of the way. And apart from everything else, wouldn't it be nice just to see old Nora again? So why not say sorry? And all said and done, that's what she'd been trying to do before that fight with Samantha.

She looked across at Mary with her row of B.A.G.A. badges showing off down her lapel. Mary was passing her note over to Sarah Longrush: some arrangements she was making, as usual, the way she'd used to do with Janey. So why not go, then? Janey thought. She'd only got her pride to lose, and that wasn't up to much these days. She slammed her book shut. And wasn't she a gymnast? Well, if gymnasts were supposed to be good at bending over backwards, she was bloody brilliant!

The extra hour of daylight gave the school a longer afternoon, working the summer timetable. Impatiently, Janey got through it, then beat them all to the school gates, couldn't wait to get down to Delaport Road. Like the first day she'd gone to do the housework, she was anxious to get over the doorstep, the hurdle, to get to grips with something, before she had time to start worrying about whether she was right or wrong to be doing it. She'd rather get on with the arrangements than worry about them: that was the difference between her and Mary.

But she didn't get near to Nora's doorstep before she found out that nothing stays still, things are changing all the time; everyone has their winters. Already things were different, and not just because she was taking a chance today instead of being invited. From halfway up the road a sign could be seen leaning out from the top of the rangy hedge: HOUSE FOR SALE: *Freehold: South East London Properties*.

Nora's place was being sold! Janey's head dropped, her hopes suddenly sucked out like pressure from a punctured canister. She ran down the pavement to make sure it wasn't next door, but it was the old woman's place all right: there were never two windows like that. Just her rotten luck! Janey stopped at the gate, which was propped open with a load of litter piled up behind it; looked beyond it to where the grass was long again with the smell of all sorts of cats' mess. Further back at the house itself the curtains were drawn and the windows were thickening with dust. She stared at it all, sick inside. There was definitely no chance anyone lived in there now. Old Nora had gone, and without ever giving her the chance to explain things. Which meant that if where she'd gone was out of reach, she'd always have it in her mind that Janey was a little crook – some council estate kid who'd conned her and stolen her precious stuff. Janey swore. Well, that was true enough for some people to say, but it definitely wasn't true for Nora: and it hurt her badly to think it could seem so.

That shut-up house could well have been the final down for Janey. After being lifted up that day from a desperate winter, after feeling hopeful enough to come and push her luck, now Janey had been slapped into her place by the sign at the gate. Disappointment is always worse after hopes have been raised. But in some weird way it didn't work like that for Janey. She *should* have been put down: she *should* have felt like shrugging her shoulders and dragging herself off home to watch the telly, with a 'Good luck!' to what anyone thought. But that wasn't what happened. Janey stood looking up at the faint sun on the stained-glass window, her thoughts still on the old lady instead of on herself, and a picture came into her head of Nora's face lighting up when she'd opened the door. She put a hand to her cheek where she'd suddenly kissed her. And right there Janey started to work out the odds.

The old girl was dead. Or she'd gone back to Canada. Or they'd moved her into a council flat. The odds were on one of those three. There wasn't much else that could have happened, Janey thought.

She leant on the gate and swung till it stuck on the path. First, then, she faced up to the thought of Nora being dead – and she threw that out straightaway. Unless she'd had some sort of an accident that didn't seem likely at all. Apart from the walking she'd been so fit, so *alive*: her old brain was so good and she had the sort of guts that never gave up. No, getting taken off somewhere seemed much more on the cards: it was what she'd been fighting against, what the others had been after, and it was definitely much more likely: getting shot off to Canada – poor old devil, imagine living with those two – or some sort of a home over here.

And it was there, leaning on that gate, staring up at the stained-glass window, that what had started out as hopeful thoughts suddenly led to the beginning of a real obsession. Never mind getting something out of it, all Janey really wanted to do was to see Nora Woodcroft or to write to her, just to tell her the truth; it could be face to face or in a note, that didn't

124

matter, just so long as she got to know it. One way or another the old woman *had* to be found; even if the worst had happened and she was no more than a name on a gravestone or in a big crematorium book like Nan Pearce. She whistled something up at the window: it seemed crazy, but with every reason for feeling down and dead, suddenly she was back in the land of the living. Out of nowhere she had a purpose.

She puzzled it out in bed, how she was going to go about it. While Reggie made the walls suck in and out with his music, Janey stared at the flaking ceiling and decided to go after school next day and talk to the people at South East London Properties. They'd know where the old woman had moved to, them and the church – but the church might have been told about Kelly, and that, Janey thought, had to make them second best.

The address was on the board: not very local, somewhere over in Lewisham – and just the sort of touch that said old Nora hadn't done it herself. You could smell the Canadians in it, picking the name with the biggest print out of the phone book; and she wasn't sure whether she was disappointed at that or not, tried not to read anything into it.

A snappy wind blew along Lewisham High Street. It watered Janey's eyes and smacked chilly round her legs. The cold yellows of early daffodils on a market stall were putting on a brave show, but it was a long way from summer yet. She caught a full-length sight of herself in a shop window – a rare view. She was scruffy and pinched and her hair was all over, not at all the sort to go into South East London Properties. If she'd had any sense she'd have phoned them, she thought. But here she was – so good luck to the lot! They could make of her what they wanted.

Thinking about it later, Janey reckoned it was a bit like walking into Brazil. It was a big place, all the ground floor knocked into one with a thick green carpet, plants growing all over the place from pots of white stones, a tropical bird cage running along one wall and a waterfall splashing into a goldfish pond in the middle. She could feel her mouth drop open, almost

hear it go. The birds were twittering and the water was
rippling: thank God they hadn't got hold of any snakes! She
looked back at the street again, tempted to go and find a phone
box after all.

"The Wimpy Bar's further along."

Janey looked at the woman who'd spoken, all Marks and
Spencer supervisor in her business suit.

"Oh, that's 'andy for you, then."

"I mean, are you looking for someone?"

Janey could see the mind working away behind the make-up.
Was Janey some cleaner's kid sent to say her mum wouldn't be
coming in tonight?

"Yeah, I am lookin' for someone, as it happens. You got a
house up for sale over Woolwich. Delaport Road. I'm looking
for the lady used to live there."

"I see. And are you a . . . relative?" the woman made the idea
sound highly unlikely.

"Yeah. Well, no. I'm a sort of a friend."

"A *sort* of a friend?"

"Well, a proper friend then. She knows me. You could tell
her my name and she'd know who you was talking about."

But the woman still didn't look very impressed. Janey could
see her wondering what she was really up to, if she wasn't a
cleaner's daughter. Checking the place out for some gang of
kids?

"I'm afraid I don't know the property you're referring to
off-hand, but as a policy we never reveal any of the personal
plans of our clients except to prospective customers." She
wrinkled her nose. "And we can't say you're a prospective
customer, can we?"

"No, we can't." Janey was getting cross now. "I just want to
know where she's gone, that's all."

"Well, I can't help you, I'm afraid. If what you're saying is
true, you'll have to enquire locally."

If! Perhaps she thought Janey wanted to find out something
to help her rob the house! All right, a few months ago and it

could have been true, but now it definitely wasn't and the idea of it made her see red.

"I'm not some crook, you know. I only want to know if she's still around."

"Our rules don't change, dear, for saints or for sinners, and my hands are tied."

Janey stared at the hard face with the put-on smile. A tropical bird started making Amazon noises somewhere over the back: and she thought how nice it would be to see an alligator come out of that fish pond and chase the woman round the desks.

"Oh, that's all right," she said, raising her voice. "I s'pose you 'ave to do what people tell you – if you're too thick to think for yourself!" She turned on her heels and went: while the woman's refined shriek of outrage shut up the jungle birds for a couple of seconds.

Outside the wind ripped harder than before. Tissue from round the market fruit blew to shop top level and tempers were frayed at the edges as people moaned at everyone else in the awkward bustle to get home. And Janey felt worse than all of them, didn't care who she knocked as she pushed her way on to a bus.

So, it was run the risk of the church, then: go and see the busybody lady who Nora had moaned about. She'd be bound to know where she'd gone, wouldn't she? The church always kept tabs on people – even when they died, especially an old people's church like Nora's. It was just fingers crossed Miss What's-her-name didn't start remembering Kelly.

The Church of the Ascension was down the road from where the old woman lived and Janey went there right away, straight off the bus. But even with the extra hour it was getting gloomy by then and the place was all locked up. Janey suddenly decided she didn't really feel like going up the spooky vicarage path and knocking on the door. Besides, she thought, something a bit more free-and-easy would suit her better: like accidentally bumping into someone where there was plenty of room to run away. So Janey saved it, and decided to go to church on Sunday instead.

As it turned out that night, she might have done better going up the dark pathway, because Reggie was prowling around when she got in, wearing a face with even more twist in it than usual, and he grabbed her at the front door.

"Come 'ere! What you up to, you?" he demanded, his teeth all bits of bread as he threw the end of a sandwich out into the long grass. "You're up to suthing, you are . . ."

Janey gave him one of her looks. "Dunno what you're on about."

"Don't give me that!" He spat food at her. "You ain't been stayin' behind for clubs I know. You're on some little game, you don't fool me!" He looked her up and down with his eyes saying all sorts of unpleasant things.

"Why don't you get lost?" she told him.

But he wouldn't go away, something else was eating at him, something he needed her for. He didn't often waste his time talking to her these days, not even to take out his spite.

"I got suthin' you gotta 'elp me with . . ."

"Why?" She badly wanted to get past him but she daren't force it: he looked ready to go off at the slightest jog, like some dodgy fuse on a bomb.

"That Kipper's really annoying me," he grated, "an' I'm gonna 'ave 'im! I am!" Violently he punched the wall a blow. He looked Janey up and down again, an open sewer stare. "I got nothin' over 'im no more, now 'e's give up that Selda. So you'll 'ave to do. You can tart yourself up an' drop the word to 'is old man . . ."

Now Janey saw what was in his mind: something to do with her letting Kipper's dad know he was playing about. "Oh no, I ain't gettin' into nothing like that. You can leave me out, son!" She said it loudly, hoping Lou might be about somewhere to come and stop all this. But the only sound in the house was Reggie snorting. He pushed her hard and made her fall up the first few stairs.

"Get this straight, you! You're gonna do *what* I say an' you're gonna do it *when* I say!" he shouted. "You're gonna do what you're told or you won't know what's hit you!" He kicked his way upstairs muttering, treading on her hand as he passed. "You got a bleedin' big lesson to learn if you think you're gonna say no to me!"

He slammed into his room and Janey picked herself up. Her back hurt and so did her hand, but it was the thought of Reggie's plan which hurt the most: a rotten scheme to sort Kipper out which meant pulling her down into his filth. Which wasn't just bad news, it was diabolical: because when he got in a mood like that nothing made him let things go.

Janey didn't go to the actual service at the church on Sunday. But she made sure she was there for the coming out, standing partly hidden by a tombstone to watch for the woman with the cape and the basket who Nora had told her about. There weren't many people to mix her up with, so it wasn't hard to spot her when she came out blinking and smiling in the sunshine: with no basket today, but wearing the cape, and a Bible held tight in her hand. She was about to turn and speak to someone when Janey jumped in fast before she lost her. "Do you know someone called Nora Woodcroft?" she asked her, straight out.

The Yorkshire sun went behind a cloud. "I know *Mrs* Woodcroft," the woman said.

"The one with bad legs?"

"Aye . . ."

"Do you know where she is, then? 'Cos I want to find her . . ."

"You do?" The woman looked Janey up and down.

"See, I'm her friend. An' I've lost touch with her, with all the cold weather an' that . . ."

"Oh. Well, I'm afraid I can't be much help, love. I know she had another fall and had to go into hospital somewhere: but

129

that was before Christmas. Went over on a glassy floor, poor thing." She was smiling sadly now, but beginning to move away. "Where she is I don't know. We lose touch, you see, if they move out of the parish: it's such a busy church here. We send flowers, of course ..."

"Yeah. Well, cheers, any'ow," Janey said, and she walked sedately away.

The stupid old trout! All over Nora one day and letting her go the next. Imagine getting to heaven and finding yourself sharing a room with her. But Nora was alive! That meant at least there was a chance! So what did you do now, then? Where did you look? It seemed stupid not to follow it up because what else was there to do? Go home and try to keep out of Reggie's way? Watch the box all day till bedtime? No, it had been good having something special to do, it had made her feel as if it was worth getting up that morning. So she wasn't giving up: not till she knew Nora was definitely in Canada: and even then she wanted her address before she stopped. Right! So how did she go about finding out where they'd taken old Nora?

Well, how did they go about finding a missing person in the police films? What did the detective always boss someone to do? Ring round all the hospitals, for a start – rule out whether they were still in one or not. And not a bad idea, Janey thought. Worth a try; except for one thing. You needed your own phone or a pile of coins to do that: and she hadn't got a penny in the world. She'd spent it all on bus fares.

But a detail like that didn't hold Janey up for long. Whether she liked it or not, robbing with Lou had rubbed a lot off on her. If you hadn't got something you thieved it or you did without. Well, she didn't have money and she wasn't going to do without: so she'd have to thieve it! With a very pious look on her face, as if she had every good intention in the world, she walked towards the church. One of the men she slipped past even smiled at her. But as soon as she had her back to them and they couldn't see her, she screwed up her face and squinted her eyes for the last few metres: another trick of Lou's to save her wasting any time, enlarging her pupils to have her eyes wide open for the dark inside the building. And sure enough, without even having to let her eyes wander, she saw just what she wanted straight away. On the table by the door sat a stack of church pamphlets: *Missions Overseas*. And standing in front of them was the small wooden box honest people put their money in when they took one. From experience Janey knew that boxes like this were usually locked away during the week: but on Sundays when people were trusted to be straight they were nearly always left about.

Well, this was all in a good cause, Janey told herself. Helping Nora after the church had left off. So taking a quick look round the building to check that no Holy Joes were still inside to watch her, Janey scooped up the box in one smooth movement and crept over to kneel low in a back pew. On the blind side from the door, shielded from sight by her prayers, she whipped a hassock from its hook in front and sat it on the box. She half stood and made the sign of the cross while she took another look around: then it was two hands on the pew in front, a light jump as if its back were the asymmetric bar and crunch down with all her weight on the hassock. Crack! It was as easy as getting into a large, thin nut. Another quick prayer and she'd got the coins in her coat pocket: after which all she had to do was put on a look of holy bliss and walk out of the church to smile sweetly back at the man.

She chose a pair of Telecom boxes by a small parade of shops. Being close to where people were about, and under the beady eyes of the shopkeepers, these were the ones that didn't get vandalized so often. Also, with two boxes side by side you could be a long time in one without having to keep blanking-off people who stood waiting.

The 'yellow pages' was there, just a few leaves unstuck, and the short list of hospitals didn't take too much finding. Three phone calls, one dead line where they'd closed another place down, and suddenly Janey was in luck.

"St. James's Hospital."

"Registry, please," she'd learnt to ask.

"Registry." Like the others, the voice sounded as if there was no way it could possibly help.

"Which ward is Mrs Nora Woodcroft in, please?"

"Who's enquiring?"

"She's my gran."

"How do you spell the surname?"

Janey spelt it, and there was a wait while someone else in the registry went rabbiting on about their night out.

"And what was the first name?"

"Nora."

" 'N' for. . . ?"

" 'N' for . . . for 'Nora'."

"Oh, yes." The woman laughed. "Woodcroft, Nora. Yes. She's in Ward 3G, love."

"Ta."

"You're welcome."

Janey slammed the phone down. Great! She hadn't hoped to get so far so quick. And old Nora hadn't *been* in 3G, hadn't moved on, hadn't gone to Canada or anything: she was in St. James's now! And today was Sunday so that meant she could go to see her. Visiting. She could catch her today while she was still in the hospital, talk to her, tell her about everything and make things right.

Janey swung out of the box and held the door open for a woman to go in. There were millions of old people's homes, she thought, council ones close by, private ones down the seaside, probably foreign ones in places like Canada. So she'd been really lucky to catch old Nora before she shot off to one of them. She could've taken quite a bit of finding once she'd gone out of the hospital, but now Janey could keep in touch – could write letters to Canada if the old lady went there, or she could visit now and then if she stayed over here. It was a really good stroke – the first bit of luck for a long time! She jingled the money left over from the church box and looked at the newsagents', to where a model spastic boy wanted money put in his head. She looked at the coins in her hands and went over towards him; then walked on past to treat herself to a couple of Mars Bars in the shop. Well, Lou was always saying it: *Charity begins at home*; and old habits died hard. Besides, it had been a hungry morning's work.

The Mars Bars filled her up: and Janey sat a long time chewing on her Sunday dinner of cheese-and-sauce sandwiches. But with the house still quiet where the others hadn't come down, she allowed herself the pleasure of letting her mind run over what was going to happen that afternoon in the hospital.

It'd be dodgy at first. When she saw her the old girl would probably pull the blanket up around her and not be at all pleased at having a little thief come to find her in the hospital. But Janey would soon get over that. She'd say one of those sayings old Nora liked, something about it not being black over Bill's mother's no more – then all in the same breath she'd tell her about Reggie and how *she'd* never robbed her, how she'd only tried to stop it, then tried to get her Rudy back. She'd pull out some flowers, give her another kiss on the cheek and say she'd clear off now she'd put things straight. Janey smiled to herself, because she knew damned well old Nora wouldn't let her do that. She'd give her a hug back and she'd probably cry, and call her Kelly, and then everything could come out. They'd have a laugh, Janey could tell her bits of news about Woolwich, ask her where she was going when she was better; and last of all, before she went, which'd be quite quick this first time, she'd end up asking her if she could keep in touch and go on being her friend.

Janey found the last bite of bread and cheese hard to swallow: not because of the Mars Bars she'd eaten any more but because of the lump which had come in her throat, something she couldn't wash away, not even with two cups of water. Poor old girl! Fallen over before Christmas and left all those months in the hospital. And she'd been such a goer, too – it didn't seem fair. But never mind. Just as long as she wasn't going to Canada

– and Janey closed her eyes and hoped to God she wasn't – no matter what, she'd keep in touch. And wouldn't it be good, old Nora and her? Janey opened her eyes and swallowed again. And she really couldn't be sure which one of them the lump had been for.

Tiptoeing about the house, Janey cleaned her teeth, did the best she could about clothes, tried to make 'Flea-bag' the last thing people would think of calling her, pulled a hard brush through her black hair and put flicks of Reggie's gel on it to make it shine. She found an old lipstick she'd long hoarded and gave her mouth a faint colouring: nothing brilliant, she wasn't any *Dallas* star. But in the end she thought she'd just about do.

Woodlands Park was the best place for flowers; she'd had many a harvest offering from the other side of the bandstand. And this year there was a sheltered part under the tall brick wall where a bed of early outdoor daffodils had shown already. With the council cut-back there were no park-keepers in sight, only owners running their dogs, and while they all walked around with their heads in the air as if the last things their dogs could be doing was having a good turn-out on the grass, it was easy, Janey found. It usually was. It didn't make it right, she knew that. She was trying to turn her back on some of the ways Lou had got her thinking, but today old Nora came first: it was all in a good cause, she kept telling herself as she floated into the park like a phantom, broke off a dozen of the best blooms and ran out through the gates like a cat. Then it was up past the cemetery, over the Common, and into St. James's Hospital: done in under half-an-hour, door to door. At the end of which Janey, flushed from her walk, happy but hesitant, found herself standing reading the confusion of signs, trying to locate the right ward. She followed the peeling arrows, a long walk through endless corridors, hurried past laundry-bags and old lifts, sniffed the dismal air of a place where people stayed without option, till she came to a walkway which led out to a line of old wooden buildings. The bulk of the visitors had dropped off by now: they'd trooped and chattered into other

134

more central places, and there was just Janey and an old man who clicked down the last slope to 3G, to the point where a smell of old dinners hit out from a trolley parked halfway across a wide door. Janey nudged it aside and marched brightly into the ward.

She'd made it. She'd got there. With her flowers still alive in her hand, she'd done what she wanted and got to the place where old Nora was.

She drew in a deep breath. Now for the big moment, that first high hurdle. Now to see the old woman after all these months. Now to find out if what she'd hoped for could happen – and if her luck had at last taken a turn for the better.

NINE

Never mind a ward: it seemed to Janey more like walking into a graveyard. The place was wide and long with beds spaced evenly down either side and white-faced old people, as quiet as the dead, buried in them. That's what stopped Janey like a hand in the face: the lack of any movement in the ward and a deep and deathly silence like a walk through Plumstead Cemetery. The old faces stared far into space, the stiff hands lay folded at rest, and the only sign of life was a solitary nurse silently entering something into a huge ledger, like some angel on the other side.

The old man who'd come in with Janey went over to where a white-haired woman was tucked tightly in bed by the door. "Hello, mate," he said in a husky old voice. She gave no reply. Her big eyes stared without blinking at the ceiling, while he carefully moved around her and arranged some flowers in a tinny hospital vase; taking out the dead and putting in the fresh.

Janey looked away. Which one was Nora, then? It was hard to tell from the door. They all looked alike, but surely to God she wasn't the age of some of these old girls! All their hairstyles were the same: white, some going bald, all cut short like prisoners. And none of them were in their proper clothes, not to make them seem like *people*: they were all in old nighties with tapes on them, and the one or two sitting out had grey towelling dressing gowns. Janey shivered. This was nothing to do with having a fall and breaking a bone, not in here. This was an old people's ward. Imagine anyone ending up in here! she thought. She wouldn't wish this on a dog. She had to be in the wrong place. That woman in Registry had given her the wrong number: perhaps it was 3B Nora was in, sounded like 3G.

But thanks to sharp eyes and a little bit of luck, a second before she gave up and started looking somewhere else, Janey thought she saw the frame, half covered by a towel, and someone who could just about be Nora sitting next to it, right down at the end of the ward. Her hair was cut short like the others but was there something about the tilt of that head? Janey took a chance and hurried on down the line. Faces turned and stared at her, big eyes in sunken sockets, open mouths in an eternal sort of surprise. She got nearer to the bed: and now she knew she hadn't been mistaken. It *was* the old lady; it was Nora; thinner in the face and wearing the same hospital clothes as the others, one hand resting quietly on the frame and the other on a closed book: but there was definitely something special about that look in her eyes: something nothing could alter – a look that was more *alive* than the rest.

Nora looked up at Janey as she approached. Janey smiled, as wide as she could, held out her flowers. She stared at the way some stranger had parted her hair on the wrong side, and "Long time, no see, eh?" she said brightly. "Remember me, Kelly?"

Nora stared at her, showed no sign of recognition, frowned.

"I'm the 'black over Bill's mother's girl', remember? The crackers for the fire? I done some work for you, we done the garden together, didn't we? Eh, you remember that?" Already she could hear herself talking in a sing-song voice, the way people talked to babies. But still Nora Woodcroft stared.

"Are you the paper girl?" The voice was high and demanding. "They don't have a proper paper girl in here." The woman stared her out, didn't seem to know her from Adam.

Janey laughed. "No, I'm Kelly – remember? I knew your Samantha." She'd ring a bell somehow, she thought, mention all the names. "You told me all about your lovely window, didn't you? An' look, I brought you these flowers. Daffs. Nice, ain't they?" She laid the daffodils on the tray, at which Nora suddenly covered her hand with her own. Janey looked into the familiar face: saw a discolouration at the top of her cheek, signs

137

of an old bruise still fading off. But most of all she looked at the eyes which were suddenly burning to tell her something.

She tensed herself, stood ready for the accusations about Reggie's thieving.

"They're very nice here, but there's a lot make trouble for them, you know," Nora said. "They won't go to sleep, some of them, they wet their beds, oh, you should hear some of the commotions!" She flapped her hands in the air. "But you bring me a paper tomorrow."

Janey tried to swallow her disappointment. She'd been ready to have the air cleared, but the way the old lady was talking she could have been anyone, as if there was nothing special between them at all. "Hold on, I'll get you a pot for them flowers. Haven't you got no drink or no grapes?" The locker top was barren: there were no comforts, not a card, not a photograph of anyone, not even of Samantha, in here. Janey went down the ward to the nurse. "I'm a friend of hers," she said, pointing to Nora. "She needs a pot for them flowers. But what's up with her? She don't seem to know me." Janey leant on the table like a consultant. Shock had made her bold.

The nurse smiled, warm and friendly. "She had a fall, darling, broke a small bone and hit her head, lost her memory."

Janey nodded. So that was it. That figured. She'd heard about cases like that, read about them in the papers. Pop stars sent them tapes of their favourite records to give their brains a push, footballers called in with cuddly toys.

"Don't no-one come to see her? What about them Canadians?"

The nurse looked closely at Janey, fingered her dangling watch as if she were weighing-up what she could tell her: came to a decision.

"You seem to know her quite well, darling. Yes, they came. And they went. But in the early days she was unconscious most of the time so the memory loss wasn't apparent . . . "

"What about some of their pictures? Couldn't she sit and look at them?" Janey had the feeling that people hadn't really put themselves out.

"Oh, we do put the pictures on her locker now and again, and when we've got time we read her the letters over. But ..." The nurse turned a page of her ledger. "Anyway, she's going to Canada when she shows some interest in getting about. They were on the phone only last week. Now her bone's mended, all she needs is some physio for her walking. They can bring her memory back in their own time, then."

"An' how's she doin' in that? She used to get about O.K., just a bit slow, like ..."

"Well, that's the problem." The nurse went back to using a more official voice. "She won't try, that's the trouble: she's given up, doesn't seem to want to know."

Janey looked round. She'd lost her memory and they'd put her in where all the others were only waiting here to die! What a way to shunt someone off! It was special help, Nora needed, Child Guidance, that sort of thing. She took the vase the nurse gave her and walked back down the ward. Poor old devil! Imagine it – her memory all out to lunch and only a few two-bob efforts being made to bring it back! She couldn't know *where* she was, whether she was on her head or her heels. If she didn't get jogged back and start walking she'd stay in a place like this for ever – or get sent to Canada and likely never catch up on who she'd been in England. All ways up it was a bit like being dead – and for a lively old lady like her!

Had they thought about getting that Ruth over from Canada again? she wondered. Had they told her how her old mum really was?

She saw to the flowers and she talked away nineteen to the dozen, putting everything familiar she could think of into the conversation. But old Nora definitely wasn't with her. She smiled and she said thank you lots of times but there was nothing at all special between them. It was as if all that nice stuff she remembered had never happened. And in the end, feeling beaten, Janey kissed her on her bad cheek, whispered goodbye, and trailed out of that depressing place.

Nora watched the girl go. What a sweet little thing, with such a lovely smile, just none too special about her clothes, that was all: but she'd forgotten to bring the papers again. She put her hand to her head. Anyway, her bad place didn't hurt any more, thank the Lord. Though where she'd picked that up was a mystery, and no mistake. If only they'd leave her alone about her walking. She was quite comfortable in her chair, thank you very much, so why couldn't they see that? And everything would come right in time. *Patience is a virtue*, she was always telling them that. She leant her head back in the chair. But you had to count your blessings: you couldn't grumble, not being looked after in a well-run place like this. When people helped you it was mean to moan: which is what made her short with some of the others. No, just let her get better in her own time and get taken back home and she wouldn't grumble. Meanwhile, she knew when she was well off and no mistake ...

Nora suddenly sat up in her chair, as if she'd been caught by indigestion. That stupid thought had just come again: that quick thought which came and went, like catching the coal-man, gone as soon as it had come. Where *was* her home if it wasn't in here? She frowned. It did puzzle her now and again. She sometimes woke in the night and had brief moments when she knew she didn't know. Then she'd drift off or they'd give her another little drink of that orange medicine and everything went lovely and drowsy again. But for the minute she was clear: just for the minute. She started staring round the ward, getting agitated.

The nurse hurried over with a little plastic pot in her fingers. "Here you are, Nora, you missed your medicine. Supper's coming up. It's no time now to start getting restless."

Nora swallowed it. It tasted lovely, made her feel good. Didn't she remember sometimes having a little secret drink?

140

But as the medicine went down, the curtain in her mind began to draw across again. Perhaps a little sleep, she thought, before they brought round the supper. That would be very nice. Now how could anyone grumble who lived the life of Riley like this?

It was all hell at home for Janey. While Nora was being lulled into a peaceful rest at St. James's, Janey was being grabbed by the throat as she came in through the front door.

"Where you been, you?"

"Nowhere. Seein' someone, that's all. None o' your business!" But the words were hard to get out with his hands round her neck.

"Your *coloured* friends?"

"I ain't got *no* friends, not coloured or nothing else."

"So where you been?"

"Why d'you wanna know?"

" 'Cos I been waitin' for you, that's why. 'Cos I got a job I need you for an' I'm waitin' to do it." The spit in his talking hit her face. "Kipper's been ridin' up an' down all afternoon on some new bike an' 'e's doin' it specially to get up my nose! So I'm sortin' 'im out. We're goin' round 'is shop today, you an' me." He pushed her away and pulled her back, rocking her head like a rag doll. "You're gonna tart yourself up rotten an' ask 'is ol' man what time Kipper's comin' out. 'E'll go spare, Kipper goin' out with some slag like you!" Reggie smiled as he relished it.

Janey found some breath from somewhere. "I ain't!" she said. "Oh, no I ain't. I told you, I got no fight with Kipper. Besides, I ain't no slag and I ain't pretending I am!"

"You bloody are if I say so!"

He shook her harder.

He was really hurting her now, making it hard to breathe at all. She could feel the stop on her throat, the blood in her face, the pressure at her temples. Already her head was going swimmy. He was choking her. "Get off!" she croaked: but still

141

he shook her, till suddenly she jacked her knee up into his groin: hard; really hard, like Samantha had done, like they showed how to do on the self-defence programmes. And then he let go. He had to. He swore, he clutched at himself, made to grab for her again – but his body couldn't make it. From his face she could see the pain just wouldn't let him do anything but hold himself. He leaned over in agony in the hallway, laying his tongue to every screamed swear word he could find. And Janey disappeared – fast, back the way she'd just come in, out through the door and down the path. But as fast as she went she'd only got as far as the gate before Reggie somehow made it to the front step

"I'm gonna kill you!" he shouted. "When you come back I'm gonna cut you up in ribbons! They'll find bits of you all over bloody Woolwich!"

"Oh yeah? You couldn't cut your own toenails!" But Janey kept on running and she only slowed when she got to the park. He'd been building up to this, had Reggie. As Lou had gone off song these past months, so Reggie had been getting taller and fatter, really finding his feet, hating anyone with more money than him, which was most people, but hating that Kipper with his business and his bikes above all. Even bashing the blacks didn't seem to be as good as getting at Kipper. Janey let out a long, sad breath. He was definitely getting worse, was Reggie. And getting worse for him meant getting more and more violent ... There was no doubt in her mind that he'd do something strong when she showed her face indoors again: it'd be a hell of a long time before he forgot that knee up the front!

Miserably, she walked round the perimeter path. The trouble was, Lou wouldn't be any help, would he? He wouldn't keep him off her, he was out most of the time – out twisting drinks off his mates, or out cold, sleeping them off. You could rely on Lou to look after you like you could rely on a slug to do you a dance. Which came down to the usual. If she wanted looking after she'd have to look after herself.

She stared round the park, pinched with the thin ruffle of a cool spring evening. The daffodils were swaying a bit, the birds making a racket before they turned in for the night. It was all right for them, but where could she turn in? that was the question. It was quite definite it wouldn't be back at her house. She'd never not gone home to sleep before, never in her life: so she could bet if there was one time Reggie would stay home to get her, it would have to be tonight. But if she couldn't go home she'd have to get her head down somewhere. She looked at the bandstand, and shivered; that was all open and bare. She looked at the shelter, its walls running like sores with what people had squirted; that was a meeting place most nights, a gang took its name from this shelter, so there'd be no kipping down quietly in there. She shivered again. The other trouble was she wasn't exactly dressed for sleeping rough, was she? She wasn't prepared: she'd run out dressed for the hospital visit.

She started to look for somewhere else, somewhere warmer. A thought passed through her mind about Mary's: once upon a time she might have gone there, spun them a quick hard-luck story. But not now, things had moved on from all that. She blew out another long breath of despair: and caught it as her mind registered the long wall she was facing, the place where the gardeners worked, where there were stacks of flower pots and greenhouses and sheds. Well, what about in there, then? Suddenly she perked up. They even had heaters in greenhouses, didn't they, keeping out the frost on nights like this? A doss down in one of them was just the job, she told herself. And the gate into the compound didn't look too high. She wandered over, pretending an interest in a scraggy row of shrubbery just by it. But she wasn't ten metres from the gate when she suddenly knew why she wouldn't be climbing over, thank you very much – not tonight or at any other time. An Alsatian dog with the fierce bark of a wolf suddenly opened up, kicking the gate towards her with the force of its meaty attack. She'd rather take her chances with an animal like Reggie than face an animal like that!

She walked back past the daffodils, looked at the place where she'd had them for old Nora, saw the thin patches like the hair on her head that time. God! she thought: that stupid fight seemed so long ago it could have happened in another lifetime. Was it only a few months? And in that moment, out of nowhere, she knew where she was going to sleep that night. Not fifty metres from where she'd had the fight: where there was an empty house she knew a million ways of getting into: where she even knew what beds were in it and which one she'd have if she could. The place that was up for sale. Nora's house, where else?

What a brilliant idea! That saying was right, Janey decided. You definitely made your own luck. If she hadn't been involved with old Nora, gone back to put things straight, she'd never have thought of this way of keeping clear of Reggie, not in a thousand years.

She ran out of the park, through the estate, and down Delaport Road, kept her fingers crossed all the way there. But when she arrived the place looked the same, the 'For Sale' sign was still up, the curtains still pulled. No-one had moved in over the week-end. Do me! Janey said.

It struck her at the gate that she could have made a mistake in her mind, imagining the place all furnished, thinking about beds – she hadn't pictured it bare boards for a second. Now she wondered about that. Perhaps the marvellous Ruth had sold off Nora's things already, made a few pence out of them and got all neat and organised for when the old girl got shot off to Canada. Well, there was only one way to find out! The answer to whether she was going to sleep comfortable or rough was to get off the street quick and into the house.

But her eagerness didn't let her training desert her. She'd treat this forced entry with all the care she'd give to a place she'd never seen before. *Not taking enough care, THINKING you know, is what gets people caught*, Lou always used to say. So without hanging about and looking suspicious, Janey pushed open the front gate and walked as bold as brass up to the front door, just the way she had that first time she called. In the porch, sad now in its cobwebs, she pushed at the bell. She cocked her head but didn't hear it ring, and took note that the little light was out. So the electricity was off. Well, what did she expect? It was a good sign, because she wanted an empty house, thank you very much.

She waited. She had her jumble sale speech on the tip of her tongue just in case. *Expect things to happen and you're done for*, Lou had always said: *you've got to be on your toes for the unexpected. Knock on the door and be ready for a gorilla to jump out. That's the way not to get caught.*

Janey knocked next, loud and echoing, but still nothing happened. She squinted through the letter box and saw the same scene as she had all those months before. An empty passage, with the hallstand still there, and a coat still hanging on it. So the place wasn't cleared out, then, it wasn't all in store. Which meant there would be a bed to kip down on!

Janey came out of the porch, and moving on as innocently as a church visitor she walked to the side gate, even hummed to herself to help her feel all above board. She tried the latch. It was locked up today: but that was only what she'd expected. Still humming, she stepped back, took an innocent 'what-a-lovely-evening' look around, and when she was sure the coast was clear, she suddenly pushed herself forward in a fast short burst.

It was all gymnastics, this. Old Mary got medals for hers and she got a night out of Reggie's reach: same skills, different prizes. Restricted to such a short run she went for the top of the gate in an upward circle, as if she were going for the high bars, kept her arms bent, took off on a good spring with both feet together and pulled her hips in close to a high front support. And it worked. The ledge of dust on the top of the gate frame almost made her lose her hold: but the movement worked. She gripped hard with her hands and scissored a leg over the top. Within seconds, still without making any noise, she was standing out of sight on the private side and giving herself a quick dust down.

Now it was get through the little window she'd spotted before and stay out of sight till the morning. She knew it was bound to be shut tight this time, but there were loads of ways of dealing with that. Quietly, she lifted the dustbin over to stand beneath the french windows. She found a brick lying loose on the top of an old, low wall: you never had to look far for something like that: and taking off her jumper, she wrapped it round the brick and climbed back onto the dustbin. Now this bit she knew all about. How many times had Lou told her? *When you don't want to break a pane of glass it's always dead easy to smash it: but when you do want to break it it's always a million times tougher than you think.* And what she also knew, because Lou had drummed it into her, was that you didn't have about eight goes at it, either: if you wanted to make people come running you made the same suspicious sound over and over; because the first time they hear something they listen, and if they don't hear it any more they relax: but the second time they hear a smash their ears are up like aerials and their hands are reaching for the phone.

She hit the window hard with the muffled brick: just one good sharp crack, longways on. The glass buckled-in like falling water and dropped to the carpet with hardly any noise at all. Just one dull smack and the slight scrape of the bin as her weight had shifted on it, that was all the noise she'd made. But still Janey froze: she didn't jump down, didn't do any more to the window for the moment. Whatever her body screamed out to do about getting out of sight, her mind trained by Lou said *wait*. The house next door was about ten metres away and was set further back from the road: it didn't actually overlook that part of Nora's garden; all the same, if the people had heard something they could easily look over from lower down and see everything they wanted. But Janey knew she had to take that gamble. Making no more noise was favourite for staying secret right then.

She counted a full two hundred, resisted the temptation to speed up at the end, until still hearing nothing from next door, she thought it was safe to make a move. Carefully putting her hand inside the jagged glass she twisted the window catch and

146

lifted the stay, pulled the broken frame up to stand balanced on the bar. It gave her just about enough room to wriggle in, she thought. As long as she kept herself clear of the bar it'd be easy as falling out of bed. But if she hit the bar, she'd get a nasty crack across the back – and stand a good chance of a gash from the broken glass. So it was down to the sort of skill she could show.

Preparing herself as she would in the gym, she took in several deep breaths and stood ready on her toes to make the next jump. It was more like an exercise on the window-bars, this one: up and through and head down the other side, grip on a chair-back instead of the proper rungs, but otherwise not a lot different. It was the sort of thing she did three times a week without thinking. Janey tensed herself: she relaxed her muscles, shook her wrists: and then she went. She jumped lightly but sure and got a good grip, pulled on her hands, took the strain on her upper arms as she ducked her head inside the narrow space, and started pushing to get her body balanced over the frame. She panted in and out to relieve the pressure of the little spike from the stay-bar as it pushed into her belly: and like that, gradually, breathing correctly, using her stomach muscles and her balance, she wormed in through the window, just brushing the bar with her bottom but without enough push to dislodge it. Down she slithered under the nets till her hands could reach at a chair back and she suddenly let herself go: plump into a cushion and a forward-roll out onto the floor. Great! No trouble at all. Old Mary would have been proud. And only then as she stood and got her brain the right way up did she catch sight of the long shards of glass in the chair crack, and think to say a quick thank you to God for letting her face miss the cut of all that.

She'd been dead lucky, she knew it, and that last bit with luck she hadn't made for herself. But there was no time for dwelling on what might have been. What was gone was gone. Without wasting a second Janey climbed back on the chair to shut the window and tidy the curtain. It all had to look normal or some

147

busybody would soon start poking their nose, you could bet your bottom dollar on that. Now, apart from a faint breeze through the break, you'd never know anything had happened. Very carefully she cleared the broken glass from the chair and the carpet, put it all in a neat pile in the wastebin, and only then, but in a hurry while there was still light, did she take a quick look all around the room.

This was the room where she'd first met old Nora, lying down there on the floor. And it didn't look all that different, either. The telly wasn't there, of course, that had been hidden away or taken back, and there was an empty-looking corner where it had been. But the main furniture was there, the sofa, the armchair, the sideboard and the big old-fashioned table with one middle leg like a tree trunk, covered with its big red cloth. The pictures were still on the walls. Janey looked at the sofa. Well, this'd do, she thought, with that red cloth on top of her she'd be quite comfy enough, if she hadn't got the guts to go upstairs.

Janey got her breath back, relaxed a bit, started to feel safe, told herself that no one in the whole wide world knew where she was right now. And that made her feel better, she was happy about that. And being a sort of visitor in Nora's house, that didn't feel so bad, either. Like that other morning in school with the reading, it had a bit of the feel of coming back where you belonged. She moved to the living room and went to look idly round the rest of the house, not the little thief any more, more the caretaker . . .

It was weird how she was always being pulled to that window. No matter what she was about there was something there which always made her want to look. At first it had been the lead in it, that's what the crook in her had seen, but for a long time now it had been the shapes and the colours in between the lead strips, the picture in the glass instead. She went quietly up the stairs in the empty house and she sat where she'd sat with Nora. It was always nice and peaceful here, she thought. The noise was all cut out, the thick carpet was soft to sit on, and specks of dust floated in the different coloured beams, a bit like the fire-fairies had. Just right for letting your brain think its thoughts about people.

About Nora, and Nan Pearce. Janey tucked her feet in and put her face on her knees, stared at the window and smelt her smooth skin like an infant at storytime. It would've been nice to live here, she thought, having some kind and proper person like Nora to look after you. Like her dad must have had with Nan Pearce. And she could guess what it would have been like for a girl like her. She'd have had her hair brushed every day, had nice clothes made, been made a big fuss of at Christmas. There'd have been laughs, and all the old sayings said as if they still counted. Janey sighed. She was all right, old Nora. And she bet that snobby daughter had never known how well-off she'd been.

Now the window was taking on that special evening look, not the same as when she'd seen it before, the sun was different this time, wasn't so red. But the picture still told the same story, old Ruth working late in the fields, breaking her back behind the proper line of women.

Janey stared, and she shivered. She could *feel* the still in the house, the sun shining the last of its warmth through the glass. It only needed a clock to be ticking away on a shelf for it to be like one of those quiet afternoons when Nan Pearce had gone up for a sleep, with everything peaceful and calm. Things hadn't been like that for ages and ages ... And silently, as if she were still trying not to wake her old nan, Janey got up and crept back down the stairs, slid into Nora's front room and stared at the fireplace. The grate was all cold now, with a fall of soot in the hearth and no crackers curled up in the basket; but the rug where they'd sat was the same.

It had been terrific, that afternoon, Janey thought. She hadn't pleased anyone so much in years as when she'd made those crackers and seen the silly fairies in the fire! It had made a real change – old Nora even giving her a hug and a kiss ...

She straightened her spine, spun round, threw herself into an

149

armchair. And it wasn't fair! Because remembering it only made her want to get hold of old Nora and hug her back like she had in the bedroom: and it made her want to cry with not being able to do it, not now the poor old girl wasn't the ticket – was all cut-off till the tape got played which'd jog back her mind.

Poor old Nora! But instead of wasting her time crying Janey looked round the room for clues to things to say: and all at once, thinking of those crackers being made by her quick old fingers, it came to her. Stupid! Why hadn't she thought of it before? She was in the right place to get hold of something here, something precious to put into her hand! That'd do the trick, that'd bring her back to the land of the living! On top of which she didn't need to give herself brain damage thinking what that something would be. It had to be Valentino. Rudy himself, if she could find him: Nora's silver dancing man!

All excited, Janey jumped up. The sudden leap made her feel dizzy and she had to steady herself on the arm: but she didn't faint, she stood still and it passed over; time to decide she was getting hungry again. She made up her mind to look for a biscuit first and make a room-by-room search for the statue after. Then if she couldn't find it – if they'd bunged it off to Canada already – she'd have to think again, find another item, but she'd get something to do the trick if it killed her!

She sat at the kitchen table with a stale biscuit from the old coronation tin and a bottle of flat lemonade. But it seemed really weird to be sitting there without the old lady there, too. It was like after Nan Pearce had died, Janey thought, sitting in her living room without the actual person who'd put it together being there to share it. You felt all out of place till you remembered how much they liked you.

She tried to relax, leant back on the chair and looked around. It was nice not having to wonder when Reggie would suddenly come up and grab her. She could sit and make her own plans.

Which she did. In a little while she'd do her search, she reckoned, then when she'd found what she wanted she'd get herself off to bed for an early night. Well, there wasn't anything else to do, was there? There wouldn't be any light left for looking at magazines, and the telly was gone, the electric turned off. She smiled to herself. It really was funny making your mind up about these sorts of things, being your own boss for a bit. But it was all right, she wasn't grumbling! She stretched her arms out wide in a big embrace. She whistled something cheerful through her teeth. It wouldn't take a lot to have her putting a note out for the milkman!

It all seemed so right and so natural that she took no notice at first of the sound of the key in the lock. For three or four seconds it didn't seem like a threat at all: in her relaxed mind it was just old Nora coming in from the shops. Then she suddenly came to. *Old Nora?* God! No! It couldn't be her! How could it be Nora? She was shut up in that hospital in no state to go anywhere!

In a rock of the chair Janey was on her feet and squinting through a chink in the kitchen door. Two men looking like policemen had just come into the hall: no hats although they had the same sort of dark uniforms. But they were talking together, laughing; not seeming as if they'd come in to catch anyone. Did that mean they hadn't come because some nosy neighbour had heard the breaking glass and phoned the police? Janey peered harder through the crack. They had something written on their shoulders: S.E.L.P. in big blue letters. She tried to work out what it stood for – and then two and two came together. The estate agents! They were minders for South East London Properties! Was that why Ruth had gone to a posh place instead of the local people?

Janey felt ice cold and calm. Tight spots like this she was used to. *Don't waste time having a panic*, Lou always said, so she didn't.

The security men had stopped by the door, were lighting up cigarettes. "Quick drag," she heard one of them say. "Then you start in the kitchen: meet you back here."

The other man grunted.

It wasn't quite dim enough for torches to come out – but the big rubber things the men carried looked as heavy as truncheons – and Janey guessed that's why they had them. Smash instead of flash!

She stood silent in the crack of the door and gently lowered the lemonade bottle to the floor. Still no panic. She wouldn't need that to help her get away because she didn't have to get past them. No, she had an easy way out: just unbolt the back door and away over the fence. They'd never catch her – not these two private plods with their fags on. But running wasn't what was going through her mind . . .

"You see that old Brando film this afternoon?" one of them was saying.

. . . She didn't have to run, not if she could stay here and dodge them. If she ran they'd know she'd been in the place . . .

"Meant to, went to kip, didn't I? Come on, then, I wanna give them new flats a quick look over 'fore it gets too dark."

. . . And there was one thing she could bet on. They'd shut this house up like Holloway then and leave her without a hope in hell of getting the silver statue. Which all came down to choosing. She could run and find some other way of keeping clear of Reggie – or she could stay and use what she knew to fool these two. And that way she might help Nora.

The younger one started coming down the passage. But Janey was already on the move – because there hadn't really been a choice at all, not in her mind. She was going to take the risk for old Nora. Across the kitchen she crept, to the hatch where she'd been surprised that day. Without making a sound she slipped through it like a magician's assistant, and by the time the security man got into the kitchen there was no sign that Janey had ever been there, unless he was exceptionally alert to fresh crumbs and the new location of a lemonade bottle.

All the same, he was pretty thorough. He even pushed open the hatch and peered through. But with a twitch of his neck like a tick on a list he closed the door and walked briskly round to the room where Janey had gone. And he was just as thorough in there. He checked behind the curtains – where the net and the gloom hid the hole in the window – and he looked behind the settee, in the sideboard, even stopped to flash his torch under the single-legged table. Then twitch and out he went to search in the room at the front. While behind him, in the dining room, Janey forced herself to count another slow twenty. Her legs and her arms and her fingers were aching ready to break; her neck, where she'd angled her head for so long, felt ready to snap, but she forced herself to wait. And only as twenty came did she slowly let herself down, seconds before she fell: painfully unwinding herself from where she'd been wrapped like a snake round the one fat leg of the table to show herself below the dangle of its cloth. Briskly, she rubbed the aches in her muscles and crouched ready to cling up again at the slightest sound of the man coming back.

But she was all right. They both went, out through the front door with a jangle of keys and the casual chat of people who don't know how well they've been fooled: and Janey was left with the run of the house, to search for that something special to jog Nora's brain.

It was in the linen cupboard: only the second place she tried, and a quick find which made her feel quite pleased with herself. What she did was put herself in the hider's shoes, in Ruth's. What would she have done, Janey asked herself, if she hadn't taken it back to Canada? She'd have put it where all the smart women with posh houses put their things. Being ever so clever they put them in their saucepans, behind their bath panels, or folded them up in sheets or towels in laundry baskets or linen cupboards. Janey had long got over being surprised at the number of times they'd found a bottle of drink, hidden from husbands and wives, deep down in some unlikely place. Vodka in the socks, sort of thing. So it was the laundry basket first, linen cupboard second, then back to the pots and pans. But the linen cupboard came up trumps. There he was, on his back, lying like a silver saint in the middle of a set of clean sheets; and almost glad, it seemed to Janey, to feel a friendly pair of hands again.

She took him out, held him, looked at him, thought of the

153

aggravation she'd had for losing him, thought of that fight with Samantha. She patted him, stroked him, spoke to him on the quiet landing. "Come on, mate," she said, "you got a job to do. You gotta do a bit of real fancy dancin' tomorrow."

And almost without thinking where she was going, but somehow knowing it all the time, she went through the doorway of Ruth's room, turned back the made-up bed, and let the warmth of her body and Rudy's start to take the chill from the sheets.

TEN

Janey went to school on the Monday. She was safer there, she reckoned, than roaming the streets with Reggie around. And she wasn't running the risk of being about if those security men checked Nora's again, not now she'd got hold of the trophy. She covered her tracks – made the bed, stuck her biscuit crumbs to a wet finger, put the lemonade bottle away – and she let herself out through a bigger and easier window in the kitchen, which she managed to leave looking shut. The Valentino she put in a plastic bag from one of the neat drawers in Nora's dresser. But she had to do without having a wash: at least, until she got to school.

Mary gave her a quick wave as she went in through the yard, and Janey waved back. It wasn't as if they were enemies: Mary just had other friends now, gymnastics club people, that was all. All the same, Janey couldn't help having a quiet smile. Mary might have all the badges for it, she thought: but she'd actually *done* more with being gymnastic. This heavy thing in her hand for a start: she wouldn't have it here if she hadn't been pretty gymnastic round Nora's last night.

All day she kept the trophy closer than a tigress does her cub. If anyone came within a metre or two her hand shot out to paw it in close. She was like a spy with a briefcase, obsessed with what was in it. Since the previous night it had become the focus of her life: not for what it was but for seeing what sort of a miracle it would work. And about that there was no doubt at all in her mind. There *would* be a miracle. Old Rudy was definitely going to do the trick: and at least Nora could go off to Canada knowing who she'd been when she was young – and who one of her real friends had been. And as for Janey after that – well, who knew? Reggie would get over his kneeing sooner or later, and then it would be back to the usual ... But at least she'd have done something she could feel proud about for once.

She ate a big free dinner, another good reason for going to school, washed where it showed in the cloakroom at break, and somehow she got through the day. She'd long since lost hold of her feelings: her stomach kept falling and churning like those first days with Lou, and she'd never known a longer afternoon in her life. But at last the clock clicked up to four, and with a wary eye for Reggie at the school gate Janey was out and running over the common to St. James's Hospital. And this time she left the flowers growing in the park, because she'd got all she wanted swinging in her bag: silver-plated Rudy, who was going to stop Nora getting old too soon, stop her sitting in her chair like the others and staring at the wall till she died.

A different nurse was on duty in the ward: a woman with more blue than white in her uniform, and Janey guessed she was a sister. Otherwise what she saw was the same as before: everything quiet and still, a woman in green trollying tea cups, and rows of white heads like seed dandelions in various stages of blowing away.

"I've come to see Mrs Woodcroft," Janey told the Sister.

The woman smiled, unexpectedly young when you got up close to her. "That'll do her good," she said. "We need more like you coming in here ..." She looked at a chart.

"I know where she is," Janey pointed. "I come yesterday."

"And you brought those beautiful daffs. She was over the moon with her flowers."

Janey's chest puffed. Well, that was something. Perhaps the old park-keeper wouldn't have minded if he'd known!

"Here, girl! Come here!" A loud female voice suddenly broke the quiet. Janey looked round. It came from the bed where the old man had been putting flowers in the vase: but the old girl was gone and a new one was sitting out in her chair.

Janey went over. "Yeah?" she asked.

"Do you know Charlie Walters?" the woman demanded fiercely, fixing her with a frightening stare.

156

"No."

"What sort of an answer's that? You could find him, couldn't you? You'd know the way to go about doing that!"

"Say 'Yes'," said the Sister. "She's gone back years in her mind."

"You could find him, couldn't you? You could ask downstairs for a start!"

"Oh, yeah," said Jenny. "'Course. I'll ask 'em for you. Charlie Walters, was it?"

"Charlie Walters," the old woman said slowly. "Tell him Ena Randall's in here."

"O.K.," said Janey.

The woman sat back and fell silent. Janey shrugged her shoulders at the Sister and walked down the ward to Nora's bed. That's how she'll turn out, she thought, sitting asking people for Alfred if she's left on her own to go potty.

The same faint smile of contentment sat on Nora's face as Janey went up. "Hello, dear," she said, as if Janey called in every day. "What papers have you got in your bag?"

Janey shook her head. She bent over and kissed Nora on the forehead. "I'm not your paper girl," she said. "I'm Kelly. Don't you remember? I know you from down your house." She stared her in the eyes, like a teacher trying to get a lesson across. "You know – your house, with your nice kitchen, 'an your hatch, an' your nice window with the picture in the glass ..."

Nora smiled politely. "Yes," she said. But it clearly meant nothing to her.

"It's black over Bill's mother's," Janey tried.

Nora looked round vaguely towards a window. "It won't rain," she said.

Now Janey stood back. All right. This was it, then. Now for the do-or-die trick, the ace of trumps. She caught her breath, felt her heart beginning to thump as she bent forward once more. "Look what I've brought you from your house," she said. Delving to the bottom of the bag she lifted out the Valentino and stood it on the tray in front of Nora. "How about that?" she

157

asked. "Your dancing man. Your statue. Yours an' Alfred's."
She stayed bending, staring, watching like a surgeon for the slightest flicker that might come on Nora's face.

It was a lot like giving a baby a toy. Not the quick grab at an old favourite, but the slow reaching out at something new. Nora's hand stretched, touched, started to stroke the trophy with her eyes fixed on it as if nothing else in the world existed.

Janey dared not move. The only sound in the whole ward was a thin rattling cough from someone near the door. Janey prayed no-one would call out. It was a must that no-one took Nora's mind off this for a minute, she told herself. Especially now her eyes were wrinkling up into a frown. She watched the fingers stroke, the forehead crease and the lips begin to move.

"Rudy," Nora said, so quietly that anyone not knowing wouldn't have made it out. "Rudy ..."

"That's right," whispered Janey. "*Rudy*. What you got for your dancing. With Alfred ..."

Now Nora looked up into Janey's eyes. "Rudy," she repeated.

"You won it, didn't you? Doin' your dancing? Eh?" And softly she hummed a few bars of dance music, as near as she could get to the tune Nora had won with.

The old woman looked up at her, a strange new expression on her face. Her eyes were alight and a question was on her lips.

"Hello, what have we got here, Nora?"

The Ward Sister kindly ruined it. She'd come up on her silent shoes to show an interest in the trophy. "A present, is it? Well, aren't you the lucky one? But I'm not sure we can be responsible for that ..."

Janey could have killed her: the woman shut Nora's face like a door slam.

"She won it dancing, with her husband," Janey said impatiently. "I was trying to jog her brain. She got the name."

The Sister wasn't stupid. "Oh, I'm sorry, love," she said, "and I came barging in." But she still talked on loudly as if Nora didn't exist. "It doesn't work like that, though. It won't suddenly come, not all at once. It does on the films, but in life it's little bit by little bit. It's not so much pulling back a curtain as doing a jigsaw." She dropped her voice. "Leave it here, never mind what I said – I'll keep an eye on it. And I'll ask doctor to leave off the sedative: we'll see what we can do between us, eh?"

"Yeah, all right. Shall I come back tomorrow?"

"No! Come back tonight, dear. Bring something else in, if you can. Keep talking to her, all the things you can think of. It might do the trick, after all, you've made a little start. One thing's for sure, love – we won't know unless we try."

"Yeah, O.K."

"We'll just leave her with this for the time being. Let her hold it till supper. Let it all sink in, give it a little bit of time. What's its name?"

"Rudy."

"Ah ..." Like a conspirator the Sister patted Janey and tiptoed away. And reluctantly, Janey went too, left Nora holding the trophy in both hands, staring at him and turning him over and over.

"Don't forget Charlie Walters!" the woman by the ward door shouted. "Ena Randall's in here, you tell him!"

"Do me best," Janey said. "Can't do no more." And that, she thought, just about said it all. Now all she could hope was that her best, as they say, was good enough.

There were only a couple of hours to wait before Janey could go back for the evening visit but they seemed even harder to get through than all the rest of that day put together: like the time spent waiting for a bus when there are no buses running, not even a full one to raise your hopes: a long, empty wait when every minute shows you how long it can be.

It wasn't as if she could pass the time by going home for a bite to eat. She still wasn't risking that, not till she could be sure Reggie was out of the way. But the chances were he'd go out

159

sooner or later, and then she could get Lou on his own and tell him: either he put a stop once and for all to what Reggie was up to or she'd push herself off into care – and take a short cut past the police station when she did it! See his face chew on all that! That ought to sort something out!

She felt hungry – it was rotten, she thought, how a big dinner made your belly want all the more. So she walked up and down the streets and tried to take her mind off it by by making up a picture of what could be happening in the old woman's ward at that moment – a sort of fantasy of hope which made the Sister all wrong. She saw Nora sitting there and looking at her old Rudy, talking to him, and telling the Sister in a sensible voice, "It's all come back to me now, dear, as clear as day. This is Rudy and I'm Nora Woodcroft and my house is in Delaport Road." Janey tripped up a kerbstone and snorted. As if! What was it Nan Pearce used to say? "Pigs might fly!"

Round and round the streets she wandered, looking in gardens, bossing through windows. She saw little kids out screeching and playing, people coming home off buses, mothers getting ratty and slamming front doors, a crowd of older kids up to something round a phone box – all the things the people who lived round there did. And she envied it: she wanted it, she'd even settle for the cusses and the clouts if she could have it. It had been good feeling normal, biscuits and lemonade without looking behind her for Reggie, having a fire and a hug, old Nora making her that little purse, her doing the gardening – and both of them knowing the old sayings. That was just about as close as she'd ever got to being ordinary like these people round here, and wouldn't she like it again!

Janey suddenly stopped in the middle of the pavement: made a man bump into her and swear. The purse! She'd forgotten about that, hadn't she? Here, what a stroke! How about the purse then? She'd left that out when she'd been thinking about things to jog Nora: her brain had gone straight to the Rudy: but the old woman had made that purse with her own hands, she'd said so. And it was plain as day when you thought about it – you

160

had to remember something you'd run up yourself, didn't you? If it was something you'd stitched and embroidered, perhaps pricked yourself with, your fingers would go back over the working like some memory you could *feel*, and they'd have to jog your brain to when you'd done it, wouldn't they? The more she thought about it the more it seemed to make a lot of sense. A big bit of Nora's jigsaw, that purse would be! She stooped to pick a snail off a wall: couldn't walk while she was thinking. So what if she went and got it, even risked going back indoors to find it? If she took that in to the hospital tonight, coming on so close to taking old Rudy, that'd be a big help to old Nora, wouldn't it? Hadn't the sister said so?

Janey thought there was every chance that it would. It was such a brilliant idea she couldn't shake it. The one small problem, of course, was getting in and fetching it: because Reggie could well be indoors for some time yet: and till Lou had been sorted out Reggie still meant murders. But she knew if she was worth tuppence to anyone she'd got to do it. Like Nora or Nan Pearce might have said, "Show 'em what you're made of, girl!" So she sat on a plank fence and went over ways of getting into her house and out without being caught.

The first thing was to be really sure in her mind where the purse was: there wouldn't be time to go hunting round for it. But she thought she knew which drawer it was in, in her bedroom. In fact she was dead certain. It was in the old sideboard she used for her clothes. She could remember crumpling it up to look more like a sock for when Reggie had his usual nose-round for something to sell.

So, knowing where it was, that just left getting in and out in one piece. And how was she going to do that? She went over all sorts of tricks, like phoning a false message to draw Reggie out: but the phone had been cut off for months, so that was put paid to. And waiting till Reggie went out on his own: but even that was taking a chance. What if Lou took his side and she had to do a run? She could end up miles off to be safe and never get back to old Nora. Besides, she had to strike while the iron was hot, she was certain of that. And she'd got in and out round Reggie before, hadn't she? So, do it dead simple, that was best, she decided. A load of speed, that was the answer, that's what she had to rely on. A quiet creep up to the front door, all slow till she got there, then in and out so quick Reggie wouldn't have time to stop picking his nose before she was away.

"'Ere, you think you're a bird, on that fence? Clear off!"

Janey looked round at the man in his vest, leaning out of his top windows. She made a sign and ran off, but all at once she felt back in the mood, the quick kid who came and went before you could catch her. And didn't she need a bit of neck to make up for the jumps she felt, doing this job? It wasn't quite the same as going out on a job with Lou, was it? Then, if someone caught her they'd just grab her and stop her: and there was tons of biting and kicking and scratching she could do to get away. But with Reggie it'd be different. After what had happened yesterday he'd half kill her if he caught her: he'd mark her, she knew that, give her something she'd carry for ever. So in a couple of minutes Janey Pearce was going to have to be slicker than she'd ever been in her life.

She turned round, saw the man still staring after her out of his window. "'Ad your eyeful?" she shouted. And her heart thumped fast and the adrenalin flowed.

Her house looked quiet enough from the end of the street. But that was nothing to go by: it was never the place for great comings and goings. Reggie *could* be out, of course, but she doubted it, not at this sort of in-between time. He'd be shaving his head or something: practising looking hard in the mirror. She pressed herself flat to the low garden walls, crouched and brushed along the bare hedges: but there wasn't a lot of cover from them. Was it really all worth it? she asked herself. After all? Wasn't the risk of being stitched a bit much for the off-chance the purse would help old Nora? Putting make-up over some scar for the rest of the life – was sending the old woman off to Canada knowing her name worth that? But Janey's feet kept moving her forward. It depended how you looked at it, who you were, she thought. Taking a chance like this was what made her *her* and not someone like Mary. The ones they called fleabags and little toe-rags, the ones like her, they were different to ordinary people. They had to be, because they knew they had more to do to get what they wanted.

She went on through next door's gate, across their front mud and up under their window where there was a gap in the palings the milkman used. She squeezed through it and came up under their own front room, listened hard, still couldn't hear a thing except the noises in the street: would have liked to put her ear up onto the glass, but she wasn't risking that!

Now she'd got to make up her mind. Not whether to go in or not – she'd already decided she was and she was sticking with it – but whether to go in by the front door or the back. She didn't need to think about it for long, though: there wasn't room for a lot of doubt: the front door was near the bottom of the stairs, while the back door, well, once you went in there you had to go through the kitchen and get past the front room to reach the stairs. And that was too chancy by miles. So, it was in through the front – and God help her if she got caught!

Creeping under the window, picking the spots for her feet where they wouldn't scrunch stones, she felt for the key on its string round her neck. Eyes all about her and ears pricked till they hurt, she drew it up slowly and felt for the ridges along the top edge. She'd only get one go at pushing it in the keyhole, no time for noisy scratching. Like a shadow thrown by headlights, she slid round into the porch. Again, a stop and a listen. She'd done nothing yet but her heart was thumping like the end of the hurdles: had to be controlled the way Lou had taught her, with deep and silent breaths. Otherwise, nothing. Not a sound.

Now she'd come to the end of the slow preparation. From here on she was going to have to be quicker than she'd ever been in her life. Once that door was open it was up those stairs two at a time, into the bedroom, pull out the drawer, grab the purse and jump back from the top of the stairs: get a good landing on the mat and shoot out through the front door again. That's the way it had to be. Anything slower than that would be death!

Right! Janey lifted herself onto her toes. She slipped the key into her mouth and put as much spit as she could make on it to help it slip quietly into the lock. All right, then. One, two, three . . .

Now!

She was going, do it or die! In went the key, good as gold. A turn to the right, slow and silent, push open the door, then up! Accelerating from nothing, Janey high-knee'd it up the stairs, pulled on the banister, pushed on the wall, made every muscle in her arms and legs work for speed and thrust. She rounded the top post, banged into her bedroom, bounced over the bed, grabbed at the sideboard drawer, pulled it out. And not listening for anything now – she was in and the whole house knew it – grab for the purse and get out.

And she had it: it was right where she'd pictured it. Six seconds she'd been, top whack. She turned, bounced back over the bed.

As Reggie from behind her door slammed it shut and stood sneering down at her.

"Oh, yeah!" he said. "Well, ain't I the lucky one?"

"What you doin' in 'ere?" Janey tried to bluster, tried to be angry, to turn it into one of their ordinary shouting matches.

"Thought you'd left 'ome."

Heart thumping, throat tight, face gone cold, Janey stared at him. He'd been looking for money again, or something to sell for glue. Or perhaps he'd been at it in here. But none of that mattered because now he was fingering his throat.

"I ain't forgot, you know. I ain't stupid. I said I was gonna teach you – cow!" With a sudden move he came at her and pushed her back onto the bed. "An' you ain't gettin' away, I tell you. An' you ain't never gonna mess me about no more, 'cos you'll remember this, madam, long as you live."

Janey screamed, forced it out high till her eyes hurt, while, terrified, they followed his hands. What was he going for? Knife

164

or belt or something else? He was shaking, smiling. She went on screaming but it was hopeless – Lou had to be out, and screams in houses round here were like dog barks.

Belt! He was pulling it out, was going to belt her first!

"Leave me be!" she screamed. "I'll kill you! Reggie!"

"Leave you be? You gotta be jokin'! You been askin' for this for years!" He had the belt out now, was wrapping one end round his hand street-fighting style with the buckle swinging.

"Get off!" Janey screamed again and made a sudden move, rolled over the bed and pushed herself down in the gap by the sideboard.

But Reggie only laughed. "You ain't gettin' away from this *nowhere*!" He swung the belt and cracked it down hard on the cushion. Janey heard the buckle tug and rip.

In a last desperate attempt she threw her head back and screamed till the scream that came out was hoarse air. But it was no good. She was trapped down there, with no getting under the bed, a sideboard too big to pull over, and Reggie blocking the door and the window. Hopelessly, she tugged at the blanket – anything was better than nothing – but Reggie had come round the bottom of the bed and was standing there watching as she pathetically curled herself up.

"You won't forget this! You won't never mess me about again!" Reggie's arm went back and his face twisted up. "You little ..."

But his arm stayed up. The blow didn't come. And Janey's terrified eyes saw a bigger grip on Reggie's wrist: the big hand of a bigger man. It was Lou, holding him off.

"Leave off, Reggie!" he was shouting. "What the 'ell d'you think you're at?" He shook Reggie's wrist till the belt dropped. Then a knee must have gone into Reggie because suddenly he danced and swung like a puppet. "You want the law round, do you?" He cracked a back-hand across Reggie's face which almost took his head off his neck.

The skinhead gave in. He had no fight in him to stand up against a man like Lou. For a second a hateful look ran through

165

his eyes. But he knew he was licked, and he whimpered. "It's 'er. You don' know what she's done!"

"Oh, no? I do know, Sunshine. She's messed me about an' all. But I'll deal with her. You keep your nose out of it! She's my business, you 'ear me?" Lou gave him a push which sent him crashing into the wall. "Go on! Out of it! You leave this to me!"

Reggie felt his way round the wall to the door. When he got it open, behind the safety of it, he found the tail-end of a sneer. "I'll 'ave 'er another time. You see!" And he slammed the door so hard Janey thought the wall would fall in. Slowly, she got up and threw the blanket off, her dry mouth getting round the words of a thank you.

But she was going to have less to thank Lou for than she thought.

"As for you," the man suddenly said, "you little madam . . ." His big hands reached out, grabbed her by the shoulders and shook her till her eyes bounced. "I'm just about up to 'ere with you, moonin' around, giving me the elbow." He hitched his trousers. "Since your madam of a mother ran off I've given you food, shelter, an' the clothes on your back. An' for what? 'S not as if you're bloody *mine*! Well, I'll tell you, Janey Pearce, I've 'ad enough!" He swung his big body round and pointed to where Reggie had just slammed out. "I swear I'll let 'im loose on you, I'll turn a blind eye next time, be somewhere else, 'less you start toeing the line!" His face came back within centimetres of hers. "You 'ear me? You start doing what I say again, you start pullin' your weight for your keep, or I'll let that animal loose on you! I will!"

Janey looked back at him. He meant what he said. He'd changed since last year, the same as her. There wouldn't be any kidding him out of this.

"An' don' start thinkin' about doin' a runner 'cos I'll get you back – an' no-one'll keep you while you've got a good 'ome." He tapped his forehead. "I know 'ow council minds work." Janey tried not to let her face give her thoughts away. "You jump to my tune, madam, an' I'll see you're all right. But give me a blank just once more an' that's it! You can run where you please, tell who you like. But it'll all be too late. You got me?" He drew his finger across his throat like some bad actor.

Janey nodded. It was all too easy to get him.

"Right!" He gripped her shoulder, hard, hurt her. "Things are gonna be a bit different round 'ere. An' for a start you can get back down them stairs an' make me a cup o' tea."

She dropped her shoulder, sighed. There was no point arguing with him. Right now he was her only protection.

Lou gave her a push, spun her onto the bed. "An' you might as well look cheerful about it an' all 'cos this is 'ow it's gonna be! Right?"

"Yeah," said Janey. "Right." And she clambered over her dirty sheets to go downstairs and do as she was told.

What a rotten world it was, Janey thought. All clever things people did, computers, and space, and stuff in the water to stop your teeth falling out, but what everything came down to in the end was, 'Can he give me a good hiding?' You could be the cleverest person in the world but if you accidentally knocked someone's drink in a pub – she'd seen it with Lou – you could well end up getting stitched. It was all down to what weapons people had – and were they built bigger than you? You didn't need school exams to survive. You needed to be big, full stop. Or rich enough to have a minder. Cavemen is what people were: still cavemen.

She cut across the common on her way back to the hospital, going through with the Nora's purse thing because it gave her somewhere to go. But she felt more down now than all through that rotten winter. Without someone to stick up for her, somewhere to go, there wasn't any way out apart from getting taken into care: and she could well believe what Lou had just told her. He'd go through the house like a dose of salts, clean it out and fool any old social worker. And then she could look out! Which left just clearing off nowhere – and who wanted to end-up dossing up west? So it was all back to Lou's ways again, it was going to have to be, because she'd suffer if it wasn't, she knew it. He'd never done nothing without her – and now he'd made up his mind she was definitely coming back!

With her head down Janey raked her way across the gravel towards the main hospital buildings. She held the purse tight in her hand, still crumpled, hadn't even had half a chance to iron it. And she sighed from the depths and kicked at a dusty stone. What was the point of ever trying anything? she asked. Some people weren't never meant to be happy.

The same Sister was on duty when Janey went in, up to her eyes with a visitor having a moan; so Janey rushed on, to get fast past the bed where Ena Randall was sitting. But tonight the loud woman was just like the rest, an empty plastic medicine pot in front of her and staring into space. Janey gave her a smile, just in case, but there wasn't a flicker of life on the calm old face. She'd probably even forgotten she *was* Ena Randall by now.

But had Nora Woodcroft remembered who Kelly was? That was the question. In a funny way, now she was here, Janey started caring about it again. Well that made some sense. Whatever had happened at home, she couldn't just switch off worrying about someone like old Nora, could she?

From her comfortable chair down the ward Nora saw fresh movement by the door: not the bash of the meals trolley but someone coming in, the little girl with the face she seemed to know. The paper girl, was it? That was the only time there was commotion, apart from the wetting at night, and when they brought round the food. Otherwise it was all very quiet and peaceful, a proper milliner's parlour. And she enjoyed her food, she told herself, she could fancy this cooking in here, brought by the ladies in green with their nice clean hands; and everyone being so kind. No, it was only the odd commotion at nights:

otherwise she couldn't wish for better. You had to count your blessings in this life. It was just that *uncertain* feeling that came over her sometimes, those little looks at somewhere else which nagged at her for a while and then went away again. It was like the sheets, out for a blow on the line. Most of the time the sheets were all you saw, but now and then a breeze popped up and gave you a look at the grass.

She rubbed her temples with two white fingers. It had usually passed over by now, this funny feeling of not knowing something. It had never lasted this long. Was it passing her by with the medicine had left her feeling like this?

Or was it something to do with this chap? Her hand went from her head to run down the smooth side of the silver trophy. 'Rudy', it was called. Oh, yes, she knew its name. It had come to her straight off, the name had. And he was a dancer; it was all to do with dancing, she knew that too, the girl had said. Which was probably why her silly old legs kept doing a jig in the bed!

And there was the little girl again, standing there, smiling at her.

"Wotcha," she was saying. "How you doing?"

Nora gave her a nice smile back. "I'm all right, lovie, I'm right as ninepence. At least, I think I am ..."

But who was she, this child? She had a very familiar face, but she said she wasn't the paper girl, didn't she? No, that was right, she was the one who'd brought in her Rudy ... But didn't she know her from somewhere else as well? Wasn't there something a little bit ... special ... about her?

"I brought you this an' all. See? You remember this? You made it for me, didn't you?"

The girl was stretching out her little hand and she took what if offered. A purse, a felt purse, and very, very familiar – made from a scrap she'd had over from ...

But just what it was *wouldn't* come, blow it. Except, "Did you put the money by?" she heard herself saying. And that was that, another silly flip of the sheets – when she'd have given anything to see a bit more – to lay a name to the girl, to satisfy herself who she was.

"That 'ouse over there, fifty-one, ain't been no sign o' life there for two days. Now, you do your best, madam – in sharpish, get a result, an' I'll buy you a nice fish supper."

"Oh, yeah?" Janey was trying to keep her spirits, but it was hard as hell. Here she was out on the rob again with Lou as if nothing had ever happened! Well, definitely nothing had got better, that was for certain . . .

She looked at the house Lou had chosen. It was a before-the-war, semi-detached, pebble-dash walls, a horse-shoe porch, and, up to now, no burglar alarm. The theory he'd bent her ears with was that its owners were quite well-off and out to work all day: the place all clean and kept-up but no-one ever about. And what he expected to get out of it was a video, perhaps a home computer, and a bit of jewellery: the sort of stuff people wanted and was nice and easy to shift.

Janey walked reluctantly up the front path and went into the porch. She hated being forced to do this, loathed having to use all her old ways to go to work for Lou again. But she had to do it and that was that: she was just too scared of him not to.

She took notice of the one clean milk bottle on a tile – then it could be just two people without any kids – and the mat with no dirt and no key under. What else? A Chubb lock, no cooking smells, no sounds – and no bell, so with a last look around and a big sigh she banged hard on the knocker. Stupid idiots! she thought. Fancy fitting a double-lock then doing nothing about an easy window next to the front door. Even Lou could get in that, blindfold!

She waited, wouldn't rush at it, wouldn't look through the letter-box just yet: she didn't want to, anyway, but she'd knock twice before she took the next step: after that, she supposed, she'd have to give that window a try. She leant on the porch, put her weight on one leg. Who'd have thought, after all she'd made up her mind about, she'd be pulling these old tricks again! Miserably, she lifted her hand to give the knocker another go: and jumped back in surprise as the door suddenly opened.

It didn't swing. It cracked open to the length of a security chain.

"Yes?" A tall woman was in the gap, old and thin and staring, with a look on her face that said as plain as day how scared she was by a knock on the door.

"Got any jumble for Gladstone School Fête?" Janey asked, jumping into her part because she had to, relieved it was all but over. But, God, what a wallie Lou was! Got it all round his neck again, hadn't he?

"When's that then, dear? What date? We usually get a letter through the door."

Blow her, the old woman was starting to take an interest. Getting the croak out of her voice. "Er, Saturday week ..."

"Saturday week?" The woman gave it a long thought. "You come back Thursday, then, and I'll look something out for you. Went to that school myself, years back ..." She relaxed just a bit as she went to close the door.

"Oh, ta," said Janey, already back on the path.

"Hold on!" The voice was as commanding as it was suddenly shrill. "Don't run away for a minute, I've got something you can take in your hand." And before Janey could put her off the face had gone from the door.

Janey looked at the sky. What was she supposed to do now? Run back to Lou for a quick get-away or stay and see it through? She usually got a brush-off when people were in, not a come-on like this. She edged back into the porch. Better hang on, she thought: with this sort of nervous old girl, if they did a bunk now she'd jump straight to her phone.

And there the phone was, all handy, right by the door on its old-fashioned little table. She inched closer. And what was that lying alongside, where someone had left it? No! How could anyone be so stupid? She blinked, but she was right, she wasn't

171

seeing things. A lady's watch on a bracelet, made of good gold. Hello! A bit tasty, that: the old girl had been phoning and slipped the thing off.

Janey listened hard, heard rummaging from the kitchen and a ratty, "Where is it?" sounding far enough and faint enough for her own hand to start reaching inside. Well, she asked herself, wouldn't it please Lou not to go home with nothing? Wouldn't it make the difference between a bad time in the car and a quiet ride back if he had a nice watch to knock out?

"Don't run away. I'll put my hand on it in a tick," the high voice called.

Me too! thought Janey, eye still on the phone table, reaching with her fingers.

"I've just lost the run of it, that's all."

And Janey suddenly froze, as still as the Rudy Valentino. *'Lost the run of it,'* the old girl had said: so why stop for that? But with her hand still half-way it came to her. It was one of those sayings, one of old Nora's: going on the hunt for her purse, that first time she'd seen her . . .

Janey whipped her hand back in disgust. So what the hell was she doing, thinking, even *thinking*, of making a grab for the watch? Had she forgotten so quick? Couldn't she still see the look on old Nora's face when she'd found something precious had gone? Didn't Janey Pearce reckon that sort of thing any more? She felt disgusted with herself. What she had to do for Lou she had to do because he was forcing her. But nicking this watch she didn't. No way. He didn't have to know the first thing about this: this was down to her!

The old lady came back, a bit more smile in the unblinking eyes. "It was in the dresser all the time," she said. "I turned it out yesterday." And she pushed a small box through the gap; which, when Janey opened it, held a glittering brooch on a cushion of old cotton wool. "It's not *good*," the woman told her, "but it might raise a few pence for your fête. Every little helps, eh?"

Janey thanked her, backed off down the path and waved her

172

goodbye from the gate, said she'd definitely be back on Thursday. And then she ran! Rotten Lou would do his nut! she knew. But blow him! She felt pleased with herself – as if she'd just passed some sort of a test.

"You're no better'n a jackdaw!" Lou grumbled when she showed him, tried to kid him about the worth of the brooch. "Give you a bit o' glitter an' you're happy." He swore a few times and crashed the gears. "If it ain't the lead in old windows, it's cheap jewellery." And the car jerked away down the road.

But he couldn't put her down with his words; and especially not now. Not this second. Because all at once the secret smile on Janey's face had nothing to do with the shiny brooch he might let her keep, not even with the pride she felt in her doorstop decision. This smile was for something the man had just said, a jog Lou'd given back to that other house – to a piece of the jigsaw she'd been too thick to see. Another up in the middle of all her downs.

What about the big window! Wasn't that one of the old woman's pride and joys? Didn't she always go all dreamy at that? All right, she told the back of Lou's neck, she couldn't hump that up the hospital. But there was a way. There had to be.

The next afternoon she didn't go home from school: Lou was sussing out another job, something round the Catholic Club, and she knew she wouldn't be missed. Instead, she stalked around the streets with a book from Miss Fairweather's classroom tucked up her cardigan. And when the time came she ran into the old people's ward, kissed Nora on the forehead, and almost pushed her back into her chair.

"Don't throw a fit but I'm gonna read to you," she said, "just a bit, something you like ..." And from where she'd been flattening her thumb in the book Janey read her piece from that R.E. lesson in the sun.

"Do not urge me to go back and desert you," Ruth answered. *"Where you go, I will go, and where you stay I will stay. Your people shall be my people, and your God my God ..."*

173

She stopped, looked at the old woman like a vicar who's finished the lesson, didn't blink, just slowly closed the book and laid it on the tray top. For a while there was silence in the ward: nothing from anyone, no coughing, no whining, no calling out; just the sound of still heads breathing out their old age. Until, undramatically, not with a shout, but in a low voice which could hardly be heard, and slowly turning her head to give Janey a smile, Nora said, "You're Kelly, aren't you?" And her voice strengthened as she said it again, "You're Kelly. Now I know who you are." She reached up with both hands and pulled Janey's head towards her. She kissed her on the forehead and on both cheeks, wouldn't let her go: until suddenly she sat back in her chair while tears of happiness ran down her face; which neither dreamt of wiping for fear of having to let go their hands.

But that was only one more piece of the puzzle. It took lots more visits to bring Nora back – after-school times for Janey between having to go out with Lou. She called them her ups and her downs – loved it with Nora, loathed what she did with the man. And the closer she got to telling the old woman the truth about things, the worse the doing them felt. It was as if she really needed the different names now, Kelly and Janey, one each to go with what she was up to, to keep the girls separate in her mind.

And she reckoned the Sister was wrong.

Bringing back Nora's memory wasn't so much like putting a jigsaw together as unravelling a tangle of string, she thought. Well, perhaps a bit of both. The window was there, and Rudy, then Ruth and Samantha came out, one sort of pulling the other: while the walking took much longer – and then not the walking itself but just seeing the need to try at it.

"Find my walking frame for me, dear," Nora asked the Sister one afternoon when Janey was there. "You're perfectly right, I've got to start doing some practice, get these daft old legs going again: because the Lord only knows what I'm doing miking about in here. I have got a home to go to, you know."

174

"Yes, we know," said the Sister. "And we can do with your bed, never you fear, we don't want to keep you a second longer than we've got to . . ." She smiled. "But there's things to sort out with Doctor first. Be patient, dear. We'll soon have you home, don't you worry." She patted Nora's hands.

"And you'll let my friend help me, won't you? I depend on young Kelly, you know."

"Oh, I think she's a great help," said the Sister. "No doubt at all about that."

Now, as the moment seemed to be getting nearer for telling the truth, Janey found it hard to look anyone back in the eye. "It weren't nothing," she said to the floor, "do it any old time . . ."

Janey told Nora the next day. Lou wanted her out with him on the Catholic Club job but she refused to go: she put her foot down, deliberately went to tell Nora on one of Lou's big afternoons. He could do what he liked, she thought, somehow it seemed only right. A sort of sign, doing it like that. Also, she knew Nora was getting nearer to coming out every day, and in the same way as she'd seen old girls disappear from the ward before, she wouldn't have been a bit surprised to go in one afternoon and find old Nora already shot off to Canada.

"Gotta go out!" she'd yelled at Lou as she'd rushed from the house. "Do it tomorrow!"

"'Ere, *you*!" Lou had shaken his fist, sworn down the road after her, told her to just wait till she got back, little madam!

But Janey's mind was made up. Before Nora went, and 'Kelly' disappeared with her, before Janey went back to being Lou's Janey, she was at least going to put matters straight. Then she'd have done what she'd set out to do: and whatever came after would just have to come.

She'd thought it would be hard: but it turned out easier than she could have hoped. Somehow Nora made it that way, sitting there smiling and encouraging and patting her hand.

"There's . . . something I got to tell you . . ." Janey began, hesitant at first, before suddenly deciding to go at it the way she'd run at a box in the gym. "See, my name ain't Kelly, never has been, not really; there's not many people call me that. See, I'm Janey to most people, really . . . "

She stopped there, froze on the box top, just to make sure her shape was all right. Nora lifted her head and nodded. I know that already, her look seemed to say: I'm only waiting for you to tell me yourself! Now that her memory was back so were the tales told by Sammy.

Janey took off again, went on and over, told her it all, went back to that first ring at her bell, through Reggie muscling in on the gardening to where she'd been taking the statue back when Samantha had kicked it.

And suddenly that was it, it was told: now she'd landed, unbalanced, only waiting to see if she'd get a hand in support.

Nora stared at her, straight. "You're not the first one, you know, lovie. You never want to think you are. I had a brother once, a proper little tear-away. Wouldn't have wished him on my worst enemy. We all get pulled this way and that, like in a blessed tug-of-war, but it's how we finish up that matters, on our feet or on our faces, that's what I always say . . . "

And now Janey knew her landing was safe, took the courage to vault over more hurdles, told Nora about Lou till the old woman sadly shook her awful, cropped head. "The devil!" she said when Janey had finished. "He wants locking up, needs putting behind bars. Can't anyone sort out the tyke?"

Janey hunched her shoulders. She was the only one: but how could she, without leaving herself open?

But she smiled. It had been good to clear the air with Nora, to have got done what she'd wanted for such a long time. And Nora appreciated it, she knew, because she'd got a warm, friendly look on her face: and a bit of that old sparkle had come back in her eyes.

The bruises Lou gave her were still on Janey's arms when they asked her to go in and see the doctor. They were hidden up under a cardigan so the man didn't see them, but after two days they still hurt if she knocked them: and they'd have been worse if Lou hadn't got Reggie to go with him and come back from the Catholic Club with silverware and drink and the cash from the machines. But she could manage a smile, said a bright "Wotcha!" when she saw who was sitting in Sister's office: lit up at the way Nora looked – all back to normal in her proper street clothes, handbag on lap, and dabbing at her nose with a lavender hankie.

"Mrs. Woodcroft specially asked that you should be here," said the doctor, as if he couldn't for the life of him see why.

"Sort of next-of-kin," said Nora defiantly. "Been such a big help to me."

Janey blushed at the praise; while Sister nodded and the doctor gave a smooth sideways dip of the head.

"We're talking around the feasibility of Mrs Woodcroft being discharged," he said, in the sort of voice Janey only heard on the telly. "And I think you've got something to say . . . " He nodded at Nora to begin the meeting, tapping his notes with a slim, gold pencil, shaking a crossed-over shoe.

Janey took her eyes off him, stared then at Nora; but she wasn't concentrating, they were well out of focus. Because while she thought it was nice, what the old girl had said, while she was over the moon to be asked into here, she knew it was all only last knockings. Old Nora would be shot off to Canada the minute this doctor said so, and that'd put the tin lid on that!

But her eyes didn't stay blurry for long. The noisy slam of Nora's handbag and the sound of her voice slapping the young doctor down sharpened them up like a stone coming at them.

"Never mind *talking about feasibilities!*" Nora started. "I'm not here for that. I'm here to tell you what *I'm going to do!* Which you can like or you can lump, as far as I'm concerned." She looked round the office like a scrapper in the playground. "Because I'm only seventy years old, that's all – and that's no age these days, am I right?" She glared at the doctor, who shrugged, tried to look like the last person who'd know. "Well, there's been presidents of America older, and Russia – and Popes! Not to mention a few judges . . . " She swung round at the Sister, who had shock still whitening her face. "And you know I'm over my fall, don't you? There's not much the matter with me now – and definitely nothing wrong up in here!" She tapped hard at her forehead. "And I'm going a treat on my frame, you must give me that." She stopped, to let what she'd said sink well in. "And now look at that lot in there!" Her voice rose again, "I ask you, you can't say I belong in with them, now can you?"

The doctor's eyes were down on his notes. He's like some old judge himself, Janey thought. He's not going to give nothing away till he says what he wants to at the end.

" . . . And no-one's going to run my life for me." Nora had dropped her voice quieter now, like the teachers did in school to keep attention. "Not Miss Stephenson, not the hospital, and not even my daughter . . . "

Janey was finding it hard to keep still. She loved a fight, a show of guts: always wanted to clap her hands or clench a fist. Now all this was getting too much!

" . . . So the first thing is, doctor, either you sign me off or I discharge myself from the ward . . . "

The doctor looked up sharply. Janey pressed herself down on her seat.

" . . . And the second thing is . . . " and here Nora took a long drawn-in breath . . . "if it's anyone's concern, I'm not budging out of my own house. I don't care what you say, I'm staying put. I won't be shunted off somewhere like a sack of old potatoes, not to Canada or anywhere else!"

A metal trolley rattled past outside, banged into a wall and made everyone look – otherwise Janey thought she'd have shouted, jumped, punched the air. *Nora wanted to stay in her house!* She rubbed the bruise on her arm which was suddenly tingling again. Was what she was hearing for real?

"Not for the Queen of England am I moving out!"

It was. And Janey's throat had choked up, was all lumped with the emotional news.

"I'm staying right here in London where I belong."

There was just nothing Janey could manage: not even a grunt to stand for all the leaping inside: she'd long since given up hope of hearing anything like this.

The doctor only managed a cough, and a nod. "The almoner has confirmed that no sale of the house has been completed," he said.

"And I wouldn't give a fig if it had!" Nora exploded. "*I've* signed nothing, *I've* not put pen to paper." She clicked open her handbag again to pull out the lavender handkerchief. "Unless someone makes out I'm mental, I can't see there's much else to say."

The doctor shook his head hard at the thought and thanked Nora for her contribution; while disinfectant and pondering hung in the air.

"Well, I'll go along with that," he said after a while, standing and flapping her notes shut. "It's certainly not our wish to stand in your way." He smiled, a very professional twinkle. "I'll sign you off tomorrow, and you can collect your pension book from the almoner." He nodded goodbye to both of them: "Good luck, Mrs Woodcroft!" and hurried off to pick up the notes on somebody else's life.

Giving Nora a squeeze, Sister followed him out. When, suddenly finding themselves on their own, all Nora and Janey could do was stare at each other like two naughty children, not sure whether to celebrate or just keep quiet about things.

"You done well . . . " Janey tried. But in the end it was Nora who found the best thing to say.

"I hope you haven't forgotten how to make crackers?" she asked.

And for another rare time in her life Janey was totally lost for words.

She bumped into Mary on her way home, rushing all important in her blazer for a seventy-five bus. "How's it goin', Mare?" she asked.

"All right, Janey. Got me gold! It's bein' engraved. How you going yourself?"

"Mustn't grumble. Worse troubles at sea."

She saw the old smile in Mary's eyes, the mates they'd used to be.

"Here, Mare, couldn't lend us two tens till tomorrow, could you?" It was on the spur of the moment, but somehow thought out all the same.

"I dunno." Mary frowned, made a show of feeling in her pockets. Then she suddenly proved the smile had been genuine. "Here y'are Janey, till tomorrow . . ." But she didn't hand the coins over till Janey had told her some more. "You ain't robbin' a bank tonight, then? That makes a change, don't it?"

"Yeah – given it up!" Janey said, straight. "Ringing the police instead."

"Stroll on!" Mary laughed, no nearer to understanding the girl.

She ran off to her gymnastics: while Janey went on where she'd just left off, forgetting her bruises for the leaps and the springs of her mind, away up the street towards the twin telephone boxes, the pair that were never out of order. She didn't know what good it would do, or even if anyone would listen to some kid's voice putting the finger on the Catholic Club job. But of one thing she was certain: from now on Janey Pearce wasn't going to be fighting her battles on her own.

*There are now around 100 titles
in Puffin Plus – some of them
are described on the following
pages.*

THE VILLAGE BY THE SEA
Anita Desai

A moving story about two teenagers facing an out-of-work father, a seriously ill mother and two little sisters too young to help or understand.

SUMMER OF MY GERMAN SOLDIER
Bette Greene

In wartime Arkansas, a Jewish girl befriends a German prisoner on the run. A most unusual and moving story.

BIKER
Jon Hardy

There's more to being a despatch rider than meets the eye! The atmosphere, speed and toughness of life riding the streets of London is captured in this fast-moving and eventful series of five episodes.

HEALER
Peter Dickinson

Pinkie Proudfoot can heal the sick at the touch of her hand. But 16-year-old Barry sees the exploitation her extraordinary talent leaves her open to, and is determined to put a stop to it. . .

ENTER TOM
June Oldham

Until now, women had been an optional extra in Tom's life, until the glamorous new Physics teacher arrives.

CLOUDY/BRIGHT
John Rowe Townsend

A sensitive and amusing contemporary love story about two young aspiring photographers. The same events are related alternately by Sam and Jenny, often from very different angles!

RUNNING SCARED
Bernard Ashley

When a sinister woman corners and threatens Paula she's pretty shaken up. Her grandfather reveals to her that he's been an unwilling witness to an armed robbery by a ruthless gang and he's got a vital piece of evidence that both the police and the gang are desperate for. Should Paula go to the cops and help expose the vicious gang? But this would endanger her family . . . Set in the East End of London, this is also a thrilling TV series.

ROLL OF THUNDER, HEAR MY CRY
Mildred D. Taylor

The Mississippi of the 1930's was a hard place for a black child to grow up in, but still Cassie didn't understand why farming his own land meant so much to her father. During that year, though, when the night riders were carrying hatred and destruction among her people, she learned about the great differences that divided them, and when it was worth fighting for a principle even if it brought terrible hardships.

EMPTY WORLD
John Christopher

Neil is alone after the death of his family in an accident. So when a virulent plague sweeps across the world, dealing death to all it touches, Neil has a double battle for survival: not just for the physical necessities of life, but with the subtle pressures of fear and loneliness.